DEVOTION

DEVOTION

Howard Norman

Houghton Mifflin Company

BOSTON · NEW YORK

2007

For information about permission to reproduce selections from
this book, write to Permissions, Houghton Mifflin Company,
215 Park Avenue South, New York, New York 10003.

Visit our Web site: www.houghtonmifflinbooks.com.

Library of Congress Cataloging-in-Publication Data

Norman, Howard A.
Devotion / Howard Norman.
p. cm.
ISBN-13: 978-0-618-73541-9
ISBN-10: 0-618-73541-0
1. Fathers-in-law—Fiction. 2. Fathers and daughters—
Fiction. 3. Husband and wife—Fiction. 4. Nova
Scotia—Fiction. 5. Domestic fiction. I. Title.
PR9199.3.N564D48 2007
813'.54—dc22   2006023454

Printed in the United States of America

Book design by Robert Overholtzer

MP 10 9 8 7 6 5 4 3 2 1

for David M.

I thank Melanie Jackson and Jane Rosenman for their close reading and encouragement.

H.N.

Devotion is a thing that demands motives.

—ANATOLE FRANCE

DEVOTION

The Accident

H ERE IS what happened. In London on the morning of August 19, 1985, David Kozol and his father-in-law, William Field, had a violent quarrel on George Street. In a café they came to blows. Two waitresses threw them out. On the sidewalk they started up again. William stumbled backward from the curb and was struck by a taxi. The London police record called it "assault by mutual affray."

This took place eleven months ago. In the intervening time David replaced William as caretaker of the Tecosky estate, near Parrsboro, Nova Scotia, on the north shore of the Bay of Fundy. William had been recovering in the main house.

Now it is near dusk on July 13, 1986. David, dressed in khaki shorts and a black T-shirt, barefoot, followed a line of nineteen swans with clipped wings up from the spring-fed pond. He wondered if there was such a word as "swanherd." He enjoyed watching each swan's awkward, comical swagger. The summer had been one relentless heat wave. David said out loud, "A swan walked right up and bit me in a park when I was eleven, in Vancouver. Maybe one of your distant cousins. Who knows?" Once David got the swans inside their pen and double-latched the gate, he walked across the lawn, wet from a fleeting late-afternoon cloudburst, the first rain in a month. Leaving footprints on the kitchen's checkerboard linoleum floor, he walked to the counter and reheated coffee. He sat at the kitchen table and continued reading *The Crime of Sylvestre Bonnard* by Anatole France, the book William's daughter, Maggie, was reading when David had seen her for the first time.

Before he met Maggie, David had fallen off reading novels. Yet he purchased nine novels by Anatole France, each a small leather-bound copy, on a single visit to the Antiquarian Muse, a used-book shop in Truro, a forty-five-minute drive east from the estate on Route 2. In June he read *The Queen Pedauque* and *Penguin Island*, often staying up through the night. Actually, he did not have the concentration or critical wherewithal to measure his level of engagement with a given novel; he only knew they kept him connected to Maggie, who, as William said, "is still your wife on paper." His reading tastes generally did not run to such philosophically leavened plots, or such noble sentiments as "the forces of my soul in revolt." Yet he had written those very words out on a piece of paper, admitting they corresponded to how he felt since the accident.

The guesthouse consisted of a kitchen, a small sitting room, a bedroom, and a utility room. It had a sloped roof with black shingles. On the fireplace mantel in the sitting room was a 1950s Grundig-Majestic turntable. David stacked records on the floor. He had come to rely on Bach's suites for unaccompanied cello, performed by the Hungarian Janos Starker. This was a utilitarian choice. David knew he was in a bad state, that every day he had to consciously work himself up to melancholy. Somehow the Bach compositions assisted in this. They allowed, as Anatole France had written of an acquaintance, "splendid companionship: my self-inflicted torment, his stark spirit." David drank too much coffee while reading. Worked his heartbeat to Morse code. What might the message be, besides not to drink so much coffee? He could not read it, an illiterate at reading his own heart.

He set down *The Crime of Sylvestre Bonnard* in order to write in his notebook. It was 3 A.M. He had come to think of it as an "if only" notebook. *If only Maggie and I had flown back together from our honeymoon to Halifax; if only, when I saw*

Katrine Novak in front of Durrants Hotel in London, I had ordered my taxi to continue on past; if only I hadn't allowed Katrine Novak up to my hotel room, William would not have found me out; if only I hadn't chased William down George Street, he would not have been almost killed by a taxi . . .

The strange thing about this notebook was that David believed everything he wrote at the moment he wrote it. Later the truth always sank in. Although he was mollified for half an hour or more by filling pages with these solipsistic equations of remorse, he finally knew that no ordering or reordering of events could save him from the effects of his own folly. Small things led to big damages — or something like that. He had badly screwed up; the steep price exacted was the ceaseless reminder of Maggie's absence. It flummoxed and pained him that his wife was not locatable, a situation he had, of course, brought on himself. He literally did not know, day to day, month to month, where she was in the world. Most likely Halifax, where she kept an apartment, but possibly somewhere in Europe, where her work occasionally took her. She was publicity director of the Dalhousie Ensemble, a faculty-student classical-music group consisting of twelve players, from Dalhousie University. His father-in-law William always knew Maggie's whereabouts, but was not telling.

He marked his place in the novels with a leather bookmark borrowed from the library in the main house. He kept

The Crime of Sylvestre Bonnard on the kitchen table. The others were in a pile on the counter next to the bread boards. *My Friend's Book, The Red Lily, A Mummer's Tale, The Gods Are Athirst, Manuscript of a Village Doctor, Patroologica.* He was grateful that Anatole France had written so many. He read by a floor lamp set next to the table. On the most sweltering of nights, if he managed to sleep at all, he did so in a chaise longue on the screen porch off the sitting room. He set up electric table fans for a cross-breeze. Often there was a mist so dense he could not see his own feet or hands when, guided by the swans' muttering, he walked to the pen and fed them dry kernels of corn. Their bills jabbed the palm of his hand, but they only meant to take what was unexpectedly offered, a kind of midnight snack.

Stefania, Isador

LOCALLY, it was known as the Tecosky estate. It consisted of 248 acres. There were few private estates of comparable size in Nova Scotia, but there was a larger one near Mabou, along the Northumberland Strait on Cape Breton. The owners of the Tecosky estate were Mr. Isador and Mrs. Stefania Tecosky, Polish Jews who had miraculously navigated the terrors of their century ("Well, it was a miracle, wasn't it?" Stefania had said. "What else could it be called, good fortune? Fortunes are for fortunetellers: liars. History is survived — that's all there is to it.") and forged a route no more or less unlikely than that of any other immigrant Jew who had entered Canada, as they had after World War II. Stefania had said, "One meaning of the word 'diaspora' is 'happy to be anywhere alive at all.'"

In 1986 both Isador and Stefania were seventy-seven years of age. Their permanent residence was on Islay — pronounced *Eye-la* — in the Scottish Hebrides. Many people who lived in Parrsboro and the neighboring villages of Upper Economy, Economy, Lower Economy, and Great Village referred to the Tecoskys as "very educated people." Dory Elliot, who owned Minas Bakery in Parrsboro, had said to David, "I miss them. They had those accents, Stefania and Izzy. It made English something different, eh? And they'd been through things in Europe gives a person nightmares even to hear about them. Nice people. Good people. Not church people of the local denomination. They knew good books and paintings and history. The elementary school in Great Village had them in as guest speakers any number of times. But they didn't bandy it about. They never overly kept to themselves nor come into town every day, and that's the way it is with lots of people around here, isn't it?"

David had his own deep affection for Stefania and Izzy. He had got much biographical information about them from Maggie, who considered them grandparents. And he'd got certain things firsthand when he and Maggie stayed in the Port Charles Hotel on Islay during their honeymoon. The

Tecoskys' house was nearby, on Upper Loch Indaal. "We've come to love Islay," Isador said one afternoon at tea. "We can't possibly consider Poland home, though we were born there. Stefania always wanted to live by the sea, but this Scottish *island?* Plenty of swans, plenty of sea birds, plenty of open space, but no synagogue! That's our little joke. After the war we wandered two years. Scotland was the first to take us in. We never forget this. Not for one day do we forget this. Memory and prayer, what else is there for us at this age? Do you see photographs of any children on our tables? No. No children. Our final resting place will be Nova Scotia. We agree on this. Many Jews went to Halifax when the war ended, through Pier 21. There were many helpful Jewish organizations waiting. In 1948 we purchased two cemetery plots in Halifax. We love Islay, but we'll finally rest in Halifax. Who could have predicted such a thing?"

In late May of 1986 the Tecoskys had visited the estate. They had come specifically to look in on William. Worried as they were about his condition. During their weeklong stay David received compliments on his upkeep of the five-bedroom main house. Each morning they had breakfast with William in his bedroom, the largest on the ground floor. David brought them tea, toast, butter, jam, and slices of melon on a tray, and left the room. Late morning, Stefania and Isador took the first of two daily naps in the master bedroom upstairs.

On their last day at the estate, David brought back the swans from the children's zoo in Halifax. The Tecoskys had waited to see this. In late autumn and winter, the swans, each identified by a thin leather collar with numbered metal tag, were featured in the indoor exhibit, which had heated pools. In exchange, the Tecoskys' swans were kept to their accustomed diet and had a pool separate from the permanent ducks, geese, and loons. Also, Parrsboro's veterinarian, Naomi Bloor, whom Stefania and Isador much admired and trusted, was allowed a monthly appraisal of the swans' health, paid for by the Tecoskys. Naomi kept a precise itemization of her expenses — gas receipts, hotel bill — on the rare occasions when she had to stay overnight in Halifax, plus the regular bill for her services.

David drove up in the estate's Dodge pickup, specially fitted with padded trailer sides and a wire cage. He let the swans loose. They headed directly for the pond, distributing themselves in four preening armadas. Their statuesque beauty. Each of their heads forming an elegant cursive S. The invisible rudders of their feet. "Since they can't fly," Isador said, "this is their great moment of freedom, I always think."

They all three watched the swans a while. "I'm remembering, just now," Stefania said. "When I was a girl, swans — from where, who knows? Norway or Sweden possibly. As a girl they would fly over my village."

William's Recovery

WILLIAM RECOVERED at a steady, impressive rate, his doctor had said. This was Dr. Rasmussen, at the hospital in Truro. Rasmussen had received all of William's medical information from London and took over. Thirty years earlier he had delivered Maggie. He was an old-style general practitioner, their family doctor. Even though she lived in Halifax, Maggie continued to consult with Dr. Rasmussen and get his second opinion on any small concern she ran past her Halifax physician, covered by Dalhousie's insurance policy.

William underwent surgery in London on August 21, 1985, which took the better part of seven hours. Before

Maggie had arrived from Halifax the day after the accident, the surgeon, Dr. Moore, spoke to David about William's condition. "His larynx is the biggest problem," he said. He had just stepped from the operating room and was exhausted. They stood in the waiting room. "His voice might return, but it won't be the same voice. The best I can come up with just now is, he might sound like the actor Peter Lorre."

"I know what you mean," David said.

"Just to utter a word or two may take a long time. Much effort. He won't have to use an electronic enhancer — that's what we call it. You've no doubt seen people holding amplifiers to their throats in order to be heard. That's positive news. He might retain a polyphonic aspect."

"Meaning?"

"It would be like, oh, I don't know, a ventriloquist without a dummy, but still managing two voices. Things will change over time, as his voice attempts the right calibration. I must warn you, Mr. Kozol, there's an outside chance the voice disappears altogether. We can't predict. We don't have the science for it. Mr. Field will need extensive voice therapy. The reasonable hope is that, given time, people will be able to understand him without difficulty."

"His other injuries?"

"Extensive. Four cracked ribs, fractured left arm. We're monitoring closely for internal bleeding and the like. But we think he'll do well on the mend. The pelvic bone's quite shattered. He won't need a new hip. But it's still a long road home."

William was sixty-one. Still broad-shouldered, he was just shy of six feet tall. He had white hair cut short, white eyebrows (his hair had turned completely white after the accident), deep crow's-feet at the corners of his dark blue eyes, tight smile and often a day or two's growth of white whiskers. "Your father's a man of substance and poise," Janice once said, rather objectively, to Maggie when she was fifteen. "Also witty and a good mind and something of a stormy temper, though I have to say, the storm usually stays offshore. Still, you can see it brewing. You're aware of it."

He was born and raised in Edinburgh, and lived there up until the age of nineteen. After a year of technical school in Boston, he returned to Scotland, where he worked as a tradesman — bricklayer, carpenter and occasional dairyman. At the age of thirty-three, on a sojourn to Gairloch to look at the cliffs and soaring sea birds, he met Janice McNeill and six months later they married there. They kept a small flat in Edinburgh, where Janice apprenticed in bookbinding. One day a letter from a Scottish friend living in Halifax included a one-paragraph advertisement for a caretaker's position, published in the *Halifax Herald*. The friend,

Richard, wrote: "Patricia and I took it upon ourselves to motor out to a lovely little village called Parrsboro and speak on your behalf to the owners, named Stefania and Isador Tecosky. We sang your praises and they were interested. So there, we've put in a good word and here's their telephone exchange. They are of the Hebrew persuasion. What's more, as blessed fate would have it, somehow after the war they landed on Islay out in the Hebrides! And that's the very reason they need a caretaker, because they're determined to return to Islay to live now."

After reading this letter, and without further need of encouragement except their own sense of possibility, William and Janice stayed up the entire night, drinking coffee and whiskey, talking about a new life. At dinner the following evening they made their first transcontinental telephone call. The conversation took about fifteen minutes. The Tecoskys agreed to provide airplane tickets ("A surprising amount of faith and generosity for just one telephone call," William commented), and a month later picked up William and Janice at the airport in Halifax.

The Fields took up temporary residence in the guesthouse. With their little savings, Janice straightaway bought tools and materials, and with the Tecoskys' permission repaired a few of the worse-for-wear books in the library, including a volume of Heinrich Heine's poems and, as Janice remarked to William in bed, "sacred Hebrew prayer books." In 1956 there were only eleven swans in residence. Over the next two weeks William demonstrated that he could handle these birds. He also oversaw the complicated task of installing a new septic system, replaced rotted sections of the wraparound porch's railing, took care of other odds and ends, some assigned by Isador, others suggested by himself.

William and Janice had not yet set foot in the main house; Stefania had delivered the dilapidated books to the front door only. But at the beginning of their third week at the estate, Isador invited them for coffee and raisin scones made by Dory Elliot. Before sitting down to talk, Stefania offered a tour of the house. The guest bedroom was on the first floor, along with the living room, dining room and kitchen, with its spacious pantry. On the dining room wall were two small oil paintings by Chaim Soutine, one of a fish, another of a garden near Paris. Neither Janice nor William had heard of this artist. Stefania took great pains to discourse on Soutine's life, saying, "He was a great Jewish painter" and "He died after surgery in 1943 in Paris." She loaned them a book of Soutine's paintings, which they looked at that same night. The library, which was adjacent to the dining room, had floor-to-ceiling bookshelves and a rolling ladder.

Then they sat down and discussed salary and other details, and at the end of this, Isador said, "We feel comfortable having you take care of this property, and we hope you'll accept. We intend to visit at least once a year, no doubt in summer, if we have the choice."

Janice said, "And we'd like to visit Scotland once a year as well."

"Two weeks vacation all right?" Isador said.

"Fine," William said.

"We have no papers for you to sign," Isador said.

"None needed," William said.

Isador went into the kitchen, brought out a bottle of champagne, said, "It's too early in the day for this, but let's make that the reason, along with our new arrangement." They each had two glasses of champagne. They talked a while longer, confident that things would work out. Then each couple, old and young, went to their bedrooms and took naps.

Stefania and Isador stayed on another month, then traveled to Islay. "Off to the next adventure, all of us," Janice said at the airport. "Bless your hearts."

Janice set up a bookbinding studio in Parrsboro, in back of a building next door to the bakery. Janice and Dory Elliot became fast friends. In fact, it was Dory's advice that Janice send notices to every church in the entire province of Nova Scotia, announcing that she "specialized" in the repair of family Bibles. Packages soon began to arrive. And for the next few years the mending of Bibles made for Janice's main-stay income.

His insurance had allowed William a private nurse up until March 1986, but then David took over those duties. He was not a poor cook, though not really inventive, which, given William's limited diet, did not much matter. He prepared and carried in breakfast, lunch and dinner on a tray. The bathroom was only a few steps from William's bed. By April William was able to slowly get into and out of bed on his own. And he had begun to take a morning constitutional to the mailbox at the end of the long, winding dirt driveway, though on William's first attempt David had found him disoriented, winded, leaning against the mailbox post, and had to assist him into the pickup truck and deliver him back to the house. Late afternoons, William might shuffle to the kitchen and make a hot cocoa. This kept his circulation going, muscles from atrophying and so on. Doctor's orders. Sometimes while watching television he stood next to the bed and walked in place. All of this was the studied pace of recovery, of getting back, as William put it, to fighting shape.

Still, William indeed spent much time in bed, watching movies on television, listening to opera — there was a Grundig-Majestic turntable in his bedroom too — the radio in general. William's pelvis had needed a second surgery, which he received in Halifax in mid-June. "This set me back," he told Maggie when she visited him in the hospital. "But it had to be done."

"You're a tough old coot. Things are working out, Pop."

His voice therapist, Dr. Marian Epson, drove from Halifax to work with him, a ninety-minute session each Monday and Friday beginning at 10 A.M. William was pleased to note she was no nonsense. In early July she had reported to William that he was "making absolutely wonderful progress. A voice more or less earns its way back through such broken architecture of the larynx. It takes very devoted labor, and some people just aren't up to it."

William thought that Dr. Epson had a way with words. He got on with her. And it was true that for him it had all been excruciating; yet each bit of progress, from a sort of whispered gargle to a few whole sentences, had been exhilarating. He had met his goal of being able, by March, to read aloud to himself from a book, twenty pages at a sitting. For this he went back to Robert Louis Stevenson. "I know they're considered mostly young people's books," he said to Maggie, "but their stories keep up with me. Stevenson's a fellow countryman. I like our reunions every few years."

William often wrote out messages rather than speak them. Those to Maggie were fatherly. Designed to exhibit humor, to let Maggie know his spirits were lifted by her presence. During his speech exercises, he'd come to understand something about the sheer physical quality of words, borne up by the industry of the voice box. *Words seem to weigh less of late* was a note he had written to Maggie.

The communications with David were quite different. On any given day they might be cordial: *We've been thrown into a strange situation here, haven't we?* Far more often, however, they had a sentiment and forecast similar to the one he'd handed to David on May 28 (David dated and filed them): *Out to the mailbox and back is seldom a problem now. Not too long, I'll be able to knock your lights out. Looking forward to the day.*

Love at First Sight

MAGGIE AND DAVID first met on April 13, 1985, in London. She was thirty, he was thirty-two. He was living in a tidy three-room flat on George Street, two blocks from Durrants Hotel, in the opposite direction from the café near where the accident took place. Yet he was often in Prague taking photographs.

At one point David had hoped to have an exhibition of his own photographs. He was part of a small group who met every Wednesday night at this or that restaurant or café, a loose-knit affiliation of photographic strivers, some very talented, all serious about the art, all quite professionally anonymous. Hoping for representation, David made the rounds of galleries, with no luck. Also, he had thought to publish a book of his photographs. No luck with publishers, either. His mentor was the Czech genius Josef Sudek. Having carried out five years of dedicated research, visited Prague dozens of times, he was something of a scholar of Sudek's life in Prague. He had visited (and photographed) every known house or apartment building Sudek lived in up to the age of twenty-five, and the shack in Újezd Street where he worked for almost thirty years. David designed a Sudek tour of Prague, parks, streets, the St. Vitus Cathedral, for his own edification. He visited private collections, pored over books and articles, even commissioned out of his own pocket a few translations of exhibition catalogues from French, Czech and Japanese. In fact, that is how he met Katrine Novak: he found her name through a Czech publishing house and hired her to translate a monograph on Sudek's early work from Czech into English.

For David, the one thing most persistent and compelling in Sudek's photographs, generally speaking, was the artist's melancholy nature, which was attested to by friends and substantiated by Sudek himself in rare interviews. Melancholy seemed the intensifying element in all of his work. David realized this was based more on subjective opinion than scholarship, but he was convinced of it. He liked to think of many of Sudek's photographs as individual frames from a Czech film noir of some fifty years' duration, each image containing a mysteriousness at once seductive to and exacting an emotional price from whoever looked at them, a price one long desired to pay in order to feel things more deeply. David felt that Sudek's still lifes especially had about them an atmosphere of intrigue, as if in the next room, or the next street over, life was perhaps not so still. He had published an article in a journal saying those very things. Though the editor praised it, the journal received no written response to David's article.

David's grandfather on his mother Ardith's side had been born in Prague. When David was eleven, his mother showed him some old, yellowed family photographs taken in Czechoslovakia — what was then part of the Austro-Hungarian Empire — in the late 1800s. David asked, "Which one is grandfather?" Ardith replied, "None — these are photographs your grandfather *took*." It proved to be a short-lived delusion, but David thought somehow his own photography might prove original enough to dignify a sense of provenance. However, after photographing in Prague whenever he could, it became evident that his work was at best second-rate Sudek, all inherited sensibility, the master's influence insistent in almost every photograph David took, even those he meditated on for weeks in advance. This was a kind of artistic malady; in effect, he could only sit next to Sudek on a park bench, stand when Sudek stood, follow a few steps behind, nod to the same passersby, similarly adjust his light meter and lens readings. A shadow photographer.

At a low point of his creative life, David, after mulling it over through a sleepless night, took it upon himself to organize his research on Sudek with the intention of writing some sort of biographical monograph or intimate study. He had always written well. This was the better choice, really. Because he had to admit that despite his technical skills, as a photographer he failed to discover an individual aesthetic. Still and all, in London he more than kept around photography. He taught a history of photography night course sponsored by the Tate Gallery. The longtime instructor, Mitchell Bowen, had fallen ill and suggested David as a fill-in. However, Bowen's illness proved more serious than anticipated; he had to retire and David stayed on.

David knew that for the Tate it was a matter of convenience, but he was determined to do a good job — to *keep* the employment. By the time he met Maggie, he was in his third year of teaching the course. Each class was comprised of fifteen students whose ages varied greatly. The course extended over two academic semesters, September through May, with the usual Christmas–New Year break. Class met from six to ten o'clock on Monday evenings. The first year of teaching, the thoroughness of David's preparation overcompensated for any ambivalence he felt, worry about getting stymied halfway through a lecture, a sense of fraudulence in the very role of teacher. The second and third years he still fiddled with lecture notes late into Sunday nights, but he was far more comfortable with the work. Critical evaluations from students were more than favorable. The Tate was pleased. David grew to enjoy the discussions, often spiced his lectures with gossipy anecdotes from his historical research and conversations with other photographers in London. Truth be told, along with his intermittent love affair with Katrine Novak and dinners with his photography group, students were David's social life. He had never thought of himself as a loner, just someone who was alone a lot. Both his parents were dead and buried, in different cemeteries in Vancouver. He had socked away their life insurance money. His steepest expenditures were on film and travel fares. He had his modest teaching salary. He liked living in London.

It was love at first sight. On April 13 Maggie had accompanied the Dalhousie Ensemble to London. It was the first stop on a six-city European and Scandinavian tour. The ensemble put up at Durrants Hotel and the next day began morning rehearsals at Queen Elizabeth Hall. It was nearly 2 P.M. and had begun raining. David was sitting in the bar just down the hall from the lobby, drinking a ginger ale to soothe his stomach. The bartender was watching a rugby match on television. At a wooden table three window washers scheduled to clean the hotel's outside windows sat in black leather chairs, smoking and talking, celebrating the turn in weather. "Nice of this rain to give us this time together, eh lads?" one said. "Let's not even suggest doing the inside windows. Let's just keep mum about that, what?" They clinked beer mugs. Their buckets and squeegees were in a corner. David finished his ginger ale and decided to head home; he'd left his umbrella in his flat. When he stepped into the lobby he saw Maggie sitting in a high-backed chair of hard red leather with wooden armrests. She was reading a book. He tilted his head in order to take in the cover and title, *The Crime of Sylvestre Bonnard*. He had not heard of the author, Anatole France. She looked up from the book, not at David, checked her watch, stood and walked outside under the awning. David immediately went there too. That is where they met, David with his jacket caped over his head, Maggie waiting for a doorman to flag down a cab.

To David, the simple fact was love at first sight. The moment provided the definition. He felt a complete realignment of emotions, along with the unbearable advance regret at not seeing this woman again. Whatever her name might be, whatever her life might be. He felt these like pangs, felt them almost hypnotically. He was prepared to get into his own taxi and despite all cinematic cliché order the driver to "follow that cab," he felt such stupefying urgency about her. If your heart is sinking you must act on it, "follow that cab," like a 1940s gumshoe trying to catch up with his own fate.

Had Maggie not paid him any mind, he might have done that very thing. He was aware, for an instant, of wanting this to be a philosophical moment, earned by years of waiting for it; wanted to maintain control of his senses. When all he really felt was apprehension and nerves and bewildering abandon, all enough to nearly render him dumb. Of course, one should never expect such good fortune. Not unless you are self-deluded beyond reason. That is just not the world. No, if it is love at first sight, you simply are in it. You cannot hope to step back and observe. His muddle-headedness was such that he could only eavesdrop on his own brain as it came up with nothing but "Hello," which he said. He and Maggie Field looked at each other's face, studied it, you might say, for just a moment.

"Actually, I can stand flirtation only in small doses," she said. "So that sufficed."

"My name is David Kozol."

A cab then pulled up. The doorman opened its back door and Maggie said, "If I want to introduce myself, I'll be back in about an hour. I'm not staying at this hotel." She then crouched into the back seat and did not look out the window. The cab moved away from the hotel.

David went back into the lobby and sat in the same chair that Maggie had. He realized that he did this on purpose. He thought, *There are other chairs available.* The man he had met earlier for lunch, portly Harrison Macomb, a publisher of coffee-table books about painters, photographers, sculptors, sauntered into the lobby. A few days before, David had arranged this lunch to discuss his Sudek monograph or book or whatever it might become. During lunch Macomb had expressed genuine interest but could not commit without a detailed prospectus. He mentioned that his daughter, Maude — "Married name Maude Harvey" — had taken David's history of photography course. "My daughter said it was occasionally brilliant," Macomb said. "I don't of course expect a book from you that is only occasionally brilliant, mind you." After lunch Macomb stayed at their table for a drink but David begged off; their conversation had twisted his stomach and he went into the bar for that ginger ale.

Macomb tucked into his raincoat, then noticed David. "Ah, Kozol," he said. "Still here, I see. My car's coming round. Drop you somewhere?"

"No, thank you. I like hotel lobbies. I'll sit here awhile."

"I'll be in touch, then. A real understanding you've got about this Mr. Sudek. We've a future together in it, rest assured."

A chauffeur-driven Bentley waited out front. The doorman escorted Macomb under a hotel umbrella the few steps from awning to curb, held open the car door. David saw Macomb tip the doorman.

Room 334

IN FACT, Maggie returned to Durrants Hotel in a little more than an hour. She paid the cabbie, got a receipt, stepped from the cab and stood on the sidewalk just to the left of the awning. She smoothed down her dress, thought, *I've worn this two days in a row now.* But if she went upstairs to change, David might notice. She might then have to say, "Well, all right, so I am staying here. But a woman today has to be careful," or something like that. What did she owe him? She did not know him in the least. It had stopped raining but still threatened rain. She saw David Kozol through the window into the dimly lit bar. He sat at a small table, a glass in front of him. When he turned toward the window (he had been turning toward it frequently) and saw Maggie, he immediately started for the lobby. She viewed what happened next as a kind of choreography, how the short-sleeved young waiter lifted David's glass and napkin, how the window washers leaned back laughing in unison, how David waved at her over his shoulder as he disappeared into the hallway. It was a view, she thought, through an amorous window.

Amorous window. The phrase derived from a concept she had read about in a Japanese novel, a philosophical love story. Back in 1983, she had fallen in love for a short time with a visiting professor of history, Shizuko Tushimo, who gave her this novel. In broad outline, the concept of the amorous window was that passion of a sudden and unprecedented intensity can imbue a window with palpable eroticism. In the Japanese story — now Maggie remembered the title and author, *The Café Window*, by Yasushi Inoue — the final irony was, years after an affair, the woman character recalls the window but not the name of her beloved. The window remains clear in her mind, rain-streaked, spectral, whereas the man in question has faded from memory. Standing in front of Durrants Hotel, Maggie, who had heretofore considered romance pretty much an abject condition, realized that no matter the outcome of her meeting with this David Kozol, she had long desired to experience an amorous window. And here, on an April afternoon in London, she was looking through one.

In the intervening time between leaving and returning to the hotel, Maggie attended to the perfunctory task of finalizing a schedule of radio interviews several of the ensemble's musicians would hold with Paul Marchand, the concert hall's publicist. Marchand would offer these to newspapers, music journals, classical-music radio programs. It was standard procedure on these tours and Maggie was very good at it. Marchand, in his early forties, was pleasant enough. His all-business demeanor proved perfect for keeping Maggie focused. Though at one point she thought, *What am I hoping will happen next?* It was a brief interlude of preoccupation, merely seconds. Snapping back to the present, she said, "Excuse me, I have to use the ladies room." When she sat down at the table again in Marchand's office, she found him putting papers into his briefcase. He looked up and said, "Actually, Miss Field, I think we've covered everything. Tea?"

"Oh, sorry, can't," she said. "I've got an assignation — appointment, I mean." The slip surprised Maggie, who felt disappointments were in direct proportion to expectations, so best keep expectations low; how certain she was that David Kozol would be waiting at Durrants Hotel. Marchand arranged for a cab.

She was not a woman who simply dropped her clothes. That was a phrase favored by her mother, who first introduced it when Maggie was sixteen and lived, of course, with her parents at the estate. It was her mother's warning, a preemptive admonishment toward any young woman, not Maggie alone, who fell to sleeping with a man before falling in love, in fact testing it with celibacy. "Marlais — your second cousin," her mother said, sighing in genuinely sad resignation, "well, Marlais dropped her clothes. Just like that. And, I heard, on more than one occasion." Hearing this in her memory just then, Maggie smiled at the endearing quaintness of her mother's exasperation and concern, let alone her phrasing. As the cab turned onto George Street and the hotel came into view, Maggie thought, *I'm thirty years old. Yes, I have dropped my clothes, perhaps twice, but mostly I have waited to know someone. Mostly. And so far I have not regretted it either way.*

Sitting for drinks opposite each other at a table in the bar, with its well-worn leather banquettes, chess and cribbage boards, scattered magazines, Maggie said, "I'm Margaret Field." She and David shook hands. He tried to take in her physical self without being obvious, but of course she detected right away and thought, *Let's just get this out of the way, shall we?* She had fair skin, a constellation of freckles on the left side of her face, a slightly denser one on the right, dark red hair, green eyes; her smile had two stages, tight-lipped to hesitantly open, and for all David knew, that might be the full extent of it. "I know," Maggie said, "you look at me and you probably think 'Irish,' huh? But my mom and dad are from Scotland. There might've been an Irish assignation a long time ago. Who knows?"

Maggie ordered a gin and tonic, two slices of lime, which she squeezed into the glass, then touched the rinds to her tongue before setting them back in. David ordered a White Russian, too sweet, but the cream in it soothed his jittery stomach. "My friends call me Maggie, but in a way, I prefer Margaret. I'm publicity director and all-around troubleshooter for an ensemble out of Dalhousie University, Halifax, province of Nova Scotia, Canada. They play classical music."

"I'm from Vancouver," David said. "Though I haven't lived there since high school."

"Two Canadians, then, having a drink together in London."

"Do you like your job?"

"Yes, I do. I do like it. We're on tour here. London. Copenhagen. Oslo. Rotterdam. So I get to see the world. I iron out all the problems. And you, David Kozol, how do you earn your keep?"

"I teach photography." He had never before defined himself like that. Or had not ever thought of himself first and foremost as a teacher. He felt a slight stab of recognition and disappointment, not that Maggie would notice. He simply wanted her to believe he had definition. Wanted her to think he was occupied in a useful manner. He hoped she would not ask if he took photographs himself, though it would be the logical question. Not ask it right away, at least. He had a book of Sudek's photographs and a half-composed letter to Katrine Novak (not a love letter: some thoughts about possible dates for his next visit to Prague — the contents could have fit on a postcard) in his leather satchel, which was at his feet.

"Kozol is what, exactly?"

"Czech. My grandfather was from Czechoslovakia. On my mother's side."

"The ensemble canceled Prague, or vice versa, I can't remember. Anyway, we aren't going there this time around."

"It's a beautiful city. Mysterious city, I think."

"I've never been."

It was surprising to Maggie, and equally so to David — each of whom did not counterfeit expectations or tailor their personalities to fit sudden possibilities — that their conversation lasted three straight hours without food and with remarkably few awkward silences. At the least, it was a welcome indulgence to both, requiring no additional drinks, either, to the annoyance of the bartender. Then the mood changed. Perhaps it was as simple a matter as a mutual sense of happiness, a lack of detected affectation, and not a little outright lustful attraction. With a relaxed, though slightly giddy aspect, there arrived a fait accompli, a telepathic decision to extend the meeting elsewhere. "My flat is two blocks away," David said.

"My room is 334," Maggie said.

They left the bar and entered the lobby. The old Italian bell captain stood at his podium near the registration desk, just in front of the wooden mail-and-key hive, which in turn was adjacent to a storage room and coat rack. Three bellmen, also Italian, at their separate stations, in the formal hierarchical configuration noticeable to any true student of hotel lobbies, as David was, did not watch directly but of course noticed as Maggie and David walked up the central staircase, with its musty-looking maroon carpet, intricate throw rugs at each landing, framed prints of zoology and botany along the wallpapered corridors. In the dusky light of room 334 (no electrical lights turned on) David sat in a pale green overstuffed chair, with its thick armrests like separate flotation devices, should the room capsize. He felt sunk down into it. "Is this the same hotel in which you always don't have a room when the ensemble's in London?" he said.

Maggie was looking out the window onto George Street. "Who's to say I didn't phone in a reservation while at my appointment?" she said. "Me being both brazen and hopeful. Apparently."

"Then I'm grateful they had a room available. It's a nice hotel. I've walked by it a hundred times."

"Never been in it, though?"

"Not till today, oddly enough."

Maggie stepped out of her shoes. "Well, here we are, then," she said. "I won't say I've not done anything like this before. Because that might sound . . . I don't know what. And besides, it wouldn't be —"

"The truth? And why should it be true, anyway? I wouldn't expect it to be true. 'Unforeseen life intervenes on regular life' — that's from a book. That's not my original thought."

"I've never done it with you before or in this hotel. *Unforeseen* —"

She then placed her shoes side by side, but in the middle of the room, smiled at David, and he thought, as comprehensively and directly as he had ever thought anything, *Where has she been?*

"Well, David Kozol," Maggie said. "You're quite handsome, but so what?"

Turning back to look out the window, Maggie thought, *Rain looks like Braille on the puddles*, to her a surprisingly tactile image, obviously one that, deep down, corresponded to how she imagined David might soon touch her. She then slid off her black stockings, reached back and unzipped her black, ankle-length cotton dress, lifted it up over her head and let it fall to the floor. (David — and it may well have been a failure on the part of his imagination — had never before fantasized a woman undressing like this in front of him, certainly had not experienced it. He recalled a phrase from John Keats, on a Poem-a-Month broadside in a London double-decker, "wild surmise," and let it articulate the moment.) She then glanced around the room, mostly taking in the quality of the light. Every inch of her body felt hastened, on the verge; also, she wished that she could impose her will on the light, somehow hurry it through dusk to dark. The streets were darker earlier than usual because of the cloud cover. This feeling must have largely been shyness, perhaps her wanting more to be touched than seen, yet every moment contains paradox, for there she was, enacting a boldness if not feeling exactly bold, slipping out of her bra and panties as David said, "I believe this could be —" *Believe*, like an act of faith. And then Maggie lay across David's lap — he saw that a spray of freckles on her chest stopped at her breasts — fell slightly back in a comic swoon, then recovered and kissed him deeply; he tasted the lime; they kissed a long time while sitting in the chair. Resting — or recovering, they did not know which — they needed to catch their breaths; she had unbuttoned only the top three buttons of his dark gray shirt but had otherwise caressed where she could reach; then Maggie said, "It so happens that next door to us, in 336, is Michael Dunbar, woodwind player. He's mostly playing oboe on this tour. He's sleeping with Marianne Brockman. She's from America. Maine, originally, I think. Miss Brockman is our principal cellist. She's in 332, also next door. You'll meet her, possibly, if we see each other past this afternoon."

"Margaret."

"Please don't fall in love with her. Miss Brockman, I mean. I'm saying it protectively. She's a bit — *unstable*. It's hard to explain, really. I think it has to do with a cellist's posture, the positioning of the cello itself. Maybe the sound of the instrument. But men, I've noticed, tend to fall in love with our cellist."

David thought that she was speaking with the utmost analytical seriousness, not at all tongue-in-cheek. This had about it a touch of didactic and eccentric reasoning, and he was interested and amused, every new thing learned a revelation. Maggie kissed him again. "Across the hall, 335, is Rachel Neiman, flautist. She's from Winnipeg," Maggie said. "Flute — I don't know why, because she plays it beautifully, but I've never warmed up to the flute. It sounds like some bird gone nuts. Rachel's very pleasant, though. I'm closest to her, of this whole group. I forgive her for playing flute."

"Let's go over to the bed."

"I just *knew* one of us was going to say that."

"You've got no clothes on, Margaret, and I have clothes on. Canadians are by nature democratic, don't you think?"

Their first time in bed together, they were at once awkward and unhurried. David undressed, pulled back the bedclothes, they lay down and held each other a few moments; David slid lower on the bed and kissed upward from Maggie's knee. That late afternoon and early evening their lovemaking was interrupted only by a shared glass of whiskey, poured from a miniature bottle provided by the hotel at cost. At about seven o'clock, Maggie rose from the bed and carried her pocketbook into the bathroom (from David's point of view, she had porcelain skin in that light), took an aspirin with a glass of water, because she knew that even so little whiskey would give her a headache, filled the glass again and carried it to David, who was parched and gulped it right down. At nine they ordered from room service, risotto and salad, but did not answer the door when the waiter knocked, and did not feel bad about it in the least. Then, around eleven, Maggie said, "I know nothing about you."

"Not a lot *biographically*, that's true. But for the last, what, six hours or so, you've learned *something* about me."

"Oh, *that*. I've forgotten everything already."

"Can you take the day off tomorrow?"

"We're in the middle of a tour here. I'm relied on."

"I don't take your job lightly. I didn't mean that. What I wanted to say —"

[37]

"What *I* want to say," Maggie cut in, "is just the time spent. To my mind it's a thing of consequence. I simply didn't need anything else."

"I do. I need to see you tomorrow."

In a short while Maggie fell asleep. David reached across and took up her book from the bedside table. He recognized the cover of *The Crime of Sylvestre Bonnard*, a Modern Library edition. The bookmark was a sheet from the notepad placed next to the telephone. He read, surprised to hear himself read aloud, in a whisper, at random from page 198: "When I returned to the City of Books I heard Monsieur Gelis and Mademoiselle Jeanne chatting — chatting together, if you please! as if they were the best friends in the world."

The passage, of course, meant nothing; all David cared about was that he was reading next to Maggie in bed in a hotel in London. He knew that had he merely found *The Crime of Sylvestre Bonnard* on the chair in the hotel lobby and read this passage, he would have closed the covers and set the book down for someone to retrieve. Yet when Maggie had, in the hotel bar, mentioned her college thesis on Anatole France, he vowed then and there to read every novel of his he could find.

He fell asleep too, and when he woke he heard Maggie speaking on the telephone: "Maybe I shouldn't have mentioned this fellow at all, Dad." The room held only the light from the streetlamps. Maggie had pulled the chair close to the French windows and was sitting with a blanket wrapped around her, facing the street. There was a pause, Maggie listening, then she said, "Far far far too soon to answer that, and trust me, it might not get answered at all, ever. On to the next subject, okay? How are the swans?" She listened for quite a while. "Poor swan," she finally said. "Poor thing — what did Naomi say?" She listened again. "Well, I miss you, Pop. I hope to see you in a week and a half, okay? When I get back to Halifax, I'll drive right out, how's that?" Then: "Great, Dad. Okay. Love you. Bye-bye, now." She set the phone on its cradle.

"Six hours time difference," David said. "Or is it five? You did say your father was living in Nova Scotia, didn't you?"

Maggie stood up, held the blanket around herself, sat next to him on the bed. "Yep, he still lives in Parrsboro, same village I was born in. I speak with my father as often as possible, David. I told you a lot in the bar, come to think of it. My lord, I told you a *lot*. I gave you an earful, didn't I? That my mother died about ten years ago, all of that. And I know I told you my dad, William Field, caretakes an estate. But I failed to mention his great love, you might call it. His great love is the swans."

"My own parents — they didn't get along, to say the least. They both died the same year, 1979, three months apart."

"I'm half orphaned, you're the whole thing."

"I've come to like swans again. I like looking at them along the Thames, or in a park, wherever."

"Again?"

"Childhood story, Margaret. I actually was bitten by a swan when I was eleven years old. In Vancouver."

"No kidding."

"Actually, it had to do with photography, in a way." Maggie turned away from David, as if allowing him some privacy in the recollection; she sensed a foreboding sadness in his shifted tone of voice; she held his left hand in her left hand at her breast. "My mother, Ardith, she used to have this phrase, 'Your father's away on business but still here in Vancouver.'"

"I take it your dad was stepping out."

"He'd stay 'stepped out' months at a time. Anyway, one morning late in the school year, the telephone rings. My mom and I are eating breakfast. She worked at Belknap Adhesives. They made masking tape, glues and pastes. Anyway, the phone rings, my mom picks it up, I'm eating my cereal, and I hear her say, 'All right, I've written that down. You understand I can't say thank you.' Then she slams down the phone. A few minutes go by and she says, 'David, when you're waiting for me after school, take some pictures of swans for me, will you?' I had this Brownie Instamatic camera. Seldom without it. So that afternoon I went to Queen Elizabeth Park, near my school. I had about ten minutes until my mother picked me up. I took out my Brownie and started to snap pictures of the swans. That's when I looked across the pond and saw my father. On a park bench. He was — how to say it? — smothering a woman with kisses. I took a picture of that. Maybe it was just an instinct to — I don't know what — maybe preserve an image that proved my dad existed or something. I was just about to snap another picture when all of a sudden this one swan charges at me full throttle. It caught me on the thumb, then gave me a good solid bite above my eye. My mom comes running up. 'Darling, are you all right?' I said a swan just bit me. She saw it happen. So I took the opportunity to say, 'When you say dad's away on business but still in Vancouver, do you mean — ?'"

"She meant what you saw on the park bench, of course," Maggie said.

"The first time I saw that photograph, it was blown up a hundred times normal size, at the hearing for my parents' divorce. My photograph as evidence."

"Your mother sounded desperate, but she shouldn't have done that to you is my opinion," Maggie said.

"Weirder yet, the woman my dad was with? Mrs. Perec, wife of our school-bus driver. Every Wednesday Mr. Perec'd detour the school bus a few blocks and stop in front of his own house. I remember the exact address was 445 Klamath Road. Mrs. Perec would step from their house dressed in a bathrobe and slippers and bring Mr. Perec a cup of coffee. All the kids on the bus thought she was pretty."

They lay there in silence. Maggie was still with the story. "Did you ever find out who called that morning?"

"Mrs. Perec. I guess she wanted it to end with my dad."

"What a shit, your dad. Sorry, I shouldn't make judgments like I do. It was probably a lot more complicated than that."

"On the telephone before, you asked your father about the swans and you said, 'Poor swan.' Sounded like there was some kind of problem."

"Oh, yes, well, a swan somehow got caught in a tangle of barbed wire. The swans don't usually wander off too far from their pond, but this one did, and there must've been some barbed wire left over from something. Hidden for years maybe in the low brush, and the swan — who knows why? — the swan got into it. My dad said he heard a distress call. Hard to describe it, but swans can sound quite the alarm. He got a wire clipper, clipped the swan out and drove it to the veterinarian's and woke her up. Her name's Naomi Bloor. She's very good at her work. Our swans are a great challenge to her. But she's learned her way around them over the years."

"How's the swan doing?"

"Recovering. Bandaged up like a World War One casualty, my dad said." Maggie pressed backward against David.

"I often think of my father as a man who talks to swans all summer long. Growing up, I heard my dad consoling or reprimanding swans in ways that had some effect."

"What kind of swans are they?"

"Mute swans. The classic-looking kind. Long, curved necks — not tundra swans. My father taught me the different kinds, from books, mainly. Their habits, migratory routes and such. It was a separate education, that's for sure. It's fair to say my dad's a self-taught scholar on swans. Anyway, the ones he takes care of are called mute swans. 'Leda and the Swan' swans."

"A girlhood spent with swans, then."

"Don't worry, I had human playmates too. I'm not — feral."

"That's disappointing."

"When I was nine," Maggie said, "I snuck around to the far side of the pond and skinny-dipped in and swam out there with a whole group of swans. That was absolutely forbidden me. Because they can get very very nasty, very aggressive. Guess I don't have to tell you that, huh? But I did it anyway."

"Ever tell your father?"

"I told my mother. She told my father."

"No family secrets, I guess."

"That time I went into the pond, I muttered and clicked and whistled at the swans like my dad does. But they kept to the opposite side, far away as possible. A few reared back, flared out their wings, and that was a little frightening, even at a distance. I remember that clearly."

"Probably your dad swam with them himself, a hot summer's day."

"Not that I knew about. Nope, I never saw him in the pond. My mother liked to swim there. Swans or no swans. When I was a kid my dad took me to the beach. The ocean was close by. This one beach near Parrsboro had shallows quite a ways out. He'd buoy me up, swirl me around, let me splash him, things like that, when I was little. What's strange is, I don't recall him actually swimming — you know, sidestroke, or backstroke, or just freely swimming along. And as for the pond, hmmm, I always wondered about whether he swam with swans out there. Now that you mention it, I bet he did."

Things Said in Sleep

MAGGIE HAD INSTALLED her father in the main house in late September 1985. He had slept through the entire flight from London to New York, slept the flight from New York to Halifax. Slept in the car to the estate. Since then, Maggie had made eighteen visits and telephoned at least once a day, even from Europe or the United States. David circled the date of each of her visits on a wall calendar in his kitchen. On all but a few of those, Maggie stayed the night in the upstairs bedroom of the main house.

Ground rules were set right away. William wrote them out:

Under no circumstances — none — does my daughter want to

see you. If possible I'll give you 24 hours advance warning of her visits. When Margaret is here, you need to be a ghost. You eat breakfast, lunch and supper at the Glooskap restaurant or the bakery or wherever. There's an all-night diner in Truro. P.S.: To my mind you're a goddamn fortunate man that Margaret's allowing you to remain her husband, on paper. For now at least.

The night of July 27, 1986, there was a cricket somewhere in David's kitchen. He thought it might be behind the toaster, or in the toaster. Or possibly in the bread box. A small embroidered Home Sweet Home pillow at his lower back, he was on page 88 of *The Crime of Sylvestre Bonnard*. It was 3:15 A.M. David dozed off, head down on the table, but almost immediately was startled awake by a sound that was at once vaguely familiar and joltingly strange. The guesthouse and pond a hundred feet away were surrounded by woods. What David heard might have been a porcupine or bobcat; they sometimes produced such eerie calls. Possibly a screech owl. He took a flashlight from a drawer, stepped out to the porch. Wild white moonlight. He hardly needed the flashlight, but he aimed it at the pen, located halfway to the pond. The swans were huddled in three groups. He recalled that Maggie once showed him an entry in the diary of an eighteenth-century naturalist named Mark Catesby: *I'm told by natives that swans mate for life. I have observed that swans have other behaviors as well.* However, none of the Tecoskys' swans were paired up. They'd arrived at the estate individually wounded.

David stepped barefoot off the porch; the cold grass felt oddly soothing. Crickets. Then David heard a rasping shriek, then an asthmatic reedy bray, and recognized the source. It was the clarinet Maggie had provided her father, on advice from Dr. Epson, to help strengthen his diaphragm, but which William also used, obnoxiously, as a kind of woodwind alarm system. David mentioned this to Naomi, who said, "Turn that clarinet into kindling. Why can't he just ring you up?"

But David was obligated here. It could be a real crisis. He was the male nurse, after all. He was the caretaker of the estate, for now. He heard the swans' wings fluttering, their jostling about the pen. William's clarinet had this effect on them. On the porch of the main house, he took the key from under the dirt-filled, flowerless terracotta vase, but remembered that William locked the place only when he was away. He opened the door and called out, "William, it's me, David!" Entering the guest room, David turned on the small table lamp near the door. He saw that the clarinet lay crosswise on the wheeled cart next to the bed. Vials of pills were lined up neatly on the cart, along with a pitcher of water and a glass. William sat upright against the headboard, watching the TV at the foot of the bed. He was dressed in long-sleeved gray pajamas.

"Looks like there's no emergency," David said.

William wrote something on a three-by-five card and handed it to David. David stepped back toward the lamp and read: *I've been thinking. I appreciate your nursemaiding me these months. But it doesn't change things. I have bad dreams about that taxi. When the right time comes, I'll knock your lights out.*

"Status quo," David said. "Well, your attitude toward me hasn't got worse. That's something."

William wrote another note. David read it: *Why not watch this movie with me. It's called Background to Danger. It started only ten minutes ago.*

David turned off the light, sat in the wicker rocking chair next to the bed. He had not heard of *Background to Danger*. Right away he saw that Peter Lorre was in it. Lorre was standing in an alley ("That guy's a weasel," William muttered) and slipping his hand into his trenchcoat pocket. He was talking to a man standing close by, whose shadow against the wall did not intervene. Close by because otherwise the knife Lorre now revealed would be of little threat. Lorre's mouth twitched a smile, then suddenly fell into a severe frown — no middle ground with this fellow. He spoke with his famous petulant, whining accent, something of a malignant Esperanto; after all, in his movies you never really knew which country Peter Lorre was from, a creepy soul without portfolio. His voice had a fingernails-on-blackboard effect. "A man betrays, he pays for it," Lorre said.

"But sometimes he gets assistance paying for it, you see. That's why I'm here. To help you pay for it." The knife flicked forward and back, and the shadow crumpled down the side of a brick building.

William had fallen asleep and was lightly snoring. David watched the movie until its closing credits and then turned off the television. He had enjoyed *Background to Danger* very much. Yet with the onset of a headache and newly jangled nerves — David suspected the cause may have been seeing Peter Lorre and recalling the surgeon's analogy in the London hospital — he realized that in all likelihood it was to be a night of wretched insomnia. While his inclination was not to try figuring out all the whys and wherefores of his frequent sleepless nights, he long ago learned to recognize their advance notices. The subtle pressure behind the eyes, the prescient slight nausea, his plummeting spirits. With Maggie on their honeymoon, he'd had three sleepless nights at intervals; Maggie had slept soundly. He told her about the problem. On a walk along the cliffs near their hotel, she said, "You also talk in your sleep, darling." When he asked what he'd said, Maggie was circumspect, mentioned just a few names. "It varies, but three or four nights, it's as if you're speaking with a Dr. Steenhagen. Does that name ring a bell?"

"Jesus, that's my pediatrician. From Vancouver."

"And what about — Dynaflow?"

David started to laugh with incredulousness. "That was my dad's car. An American car, a Buick, Dynaflow transmission. I was always begging my mom to let me sleep in the Buick on summer nights."

"Did she let you?"

"Once or twice."

"Well, you must be dreaming of this Dr. Steenhagen and that car, David. That's all I know."

"Do I keep you awake?"

"I eavesdrop a few minutes, then nod right off. Maybe that's selfish, huh? Should I wake you?"

"Why both not sleep?"

"They say if you talk talk talk a troubling thing out, you might make all sorts of connections. I suppose that's Freud in a nutshell. But you know what I mean."

David knew the connection between Dr. Steenhagen and the Buick. He regretted not informing Maggie about it then and there. (He thought: *What kind of choice was that, either not sleep or talk in your sleep, on one's honeymoon? Did Maggie now think she was in for a lifetime of this?*) After his parents' divorce, he started having what Dr. Steenhagen called "nervous stomach." It kept him awake at night. His mother made an appointment. When asked what she thought might be the source of the problem, she said, "Well, I think one culprit's David's cursive example."

Students worked on their "cursive example" every Thursday morning. Blue, wide-lined notebooks were handed front to back down the aisles of standard Canadian school desks, pencils were distributed, and then David's fifth-form teacher, Mrs. Dhomhnaill, would say, "Here is today's paragraph. It's from *The Pickwick Papers* by Charles Dickens," or some other famous book. She'd read the paragraph with glacial deliberation, allowing the students to take dictation, the entire class transformed into stenographers. "You have two minutes by the clock to hand in your examples."

In Mrs. Dhomhnaill's view — she sent home weekly reports — David's *l*'s looped too widely, his *b*'s were erratic, his *z*'s shopworn. David admitted that she had an inventive vocabulary when describing flaws in a student's handwriting. She didn't regularly single David out in her critiques, though once she flapped his open notebook in midair, saying, "Now this is a *cursed* example!"

"What are the symptoms again?" Dr. Steenhagen said.

"Stomach clenches up. Headaches, sometimes. Can't sleep the night before, like I said."

"Have you discussed this with his teacher?"

"I don't wish to embarrass my son."

Dr. Steenhagen turned to David in the examination room. "Son," he said, "there's nothing to be embarrassed about. You can't be good at everything. You're very good with a camera, your mother tells me. Look at *my* handwriting." He showed David a scribbled notation on a prescription pad.

"See, I've done all right in life, and my handwriting's like barbed wire."

Humiliated as he was, this made David laugh. He looked out the window at the family car in the parking lot. He wanted to take a nap in it. Dr. Steenhagen followed David's gaze. "Isn't that your Buick, Mrs. Kozol?" he said.

"Yes, it is."

"Beautiful automobile. Smooth ride, I bet. It's what, about ten years old? Let's go out and have a look, shall we?"

Puzzled, they followed him through the waiting room and out to the lot. He had his stethoscope around his neck. When they got to the car, he opened the passenger-side door and leaned in. He whistled appreciatively at the plush interior, then took note of the word "Dynaflow," which moved in elegant silver-metal cursive across the dashboard. "Just as I thought," he said, as if making a diagnosis. "David, do me a favor. Sit in the front seat here." David looked to his mother for permission; Ardith smiled and nodded yes. David slid into the front seat. "Now, David, close your eyes," Dr. Steenhagen said. "That's good. Now, I'm going to lift your hand to the dashboard. Okay, feel the metal writing? That's Dynaflow" — he elongated the word like a TV sales pitch. "You must've read it a million times, right?" He let go of David's hand. "You run your pointer-finger over it a few more times. Then open your eyes."

When David opened his eyes, he stared at the word, really

seeing it for the first time. "Since your son's nemesis seems to be his cursive example," Dr. Steenhagen said, "well, practice makes perfect." David got out of the car. Dr. Steenhagen put his hands on David's shoulders, looked him straight in the eye. "Here's some advice from your family doctor, young man. When you get home, sit in the front seat of this car and take out a pencil and paper and copy out the word 'Dynaflow,' oh, let's say one hundred times. You saw how perfectly it's written on the dashboard. I guarantee, if you do this every day for a week, you'll get a tenfold improvement in your cursive example, maybe twentyfold."

It did not strike Ardith as plausible advice, but it was doctor's advice, and David took it to heart. This appointment was on a Friday. As it happened, between Friday evening and the following Wednesday evening David wrote "Dynaflow," by his own count (using ⧺⧺ to represent 5), 1,015 times. The middle finger of his right hand formed a callus, actually bruised up a little. He experienced only the mildest hint of nervous stomach Wednesday night, took some Pepto Bismol and slept for six hours, until Ardith woke him for breakfast.

The problem was, "Dynaflow" was rooted so deeply in his mind that when that week's cursive example took place, David unconsciously inserted it midsentence in a dictated paragraph from the Book of Genesis. Reviewing the collective examples while the students did arithmetic problems,

Mrs. Dhomhnaill was duly impressed to see how much David's handwriting had improved. On the other hand, she was perplexed by his inclusion of "Dynaflow" (whose common usage was unknown to her). She decided not to address it with David but to subtract half a grade. He received an A-minus.

The swans had settled down. Back in the guesthouse, David percolated coffee. He wrote in his notebook, *If I'd been devoted to my marriage, I would not have* —, stared at the page until the coffee was ready. He sat on the porch sipping coffee. He went back to the kitchen, closed the notebook, took up *The Crime of Sylvestre Bonnard*. His headache spiked in intensity two or three times but otherwise was manageable, and it disappeared by 5:15 in the morning, just as he finished the novel.

He then stood at the open screen door and stared out at the darkness, now filtering a little dawn light through the mist. He reached into the back pocket of his khaki shorts, removing the photograph the doorman had taken of him and Maggie together in front of Durrants Hotel the first morning they spent together, more than a year ago. In the photograph, David looked disheveled, harried; he was touching Maggie's hand, not holding it; Maggie's eyes were somewhat squinted up; she looked breezy, alert and pleased. They were more huddled together than embracing, but definitely out in public together, in the sunlight after a night of rain.

David slid the photograph back inside the transparent plastic pocket, set the wallet on top of the peaches, pears and apples in a bright yellow bowl on the kitchen table. This was where he always put his wallet, in that bowl. It had become habit. *Now, which one next?* he thought, approaching the stack of novels on the counter. He ran his finger along the spines, then pulled *Manuscript of a Country Doctor* out, immediately balancing the others in their column. *Maggie told me this was one of her favorites.*

Room 334

THE DOORMAN WHO had taken their photograph was named John Franco. That morning, Maggie handed him her pocket-size tourist camera. John Franco snapped a picture, then opened his palm for a tip. "Joking," he said when Maggie narrowed her eyes and took back the camera. Ever alert, he turned to another couple getting out of a taxi; the trunk popped open and John Franco lifted out two suitcases. Maggie put her camera in her Dutch schoolbag. She and David went back inside the hotel to have breakfast.

It was 9:30 A.M. They had slept later than either had done in years, though they'd been awake, except for brief naps, until dawn. In the dining room an Indian woman sat alone reading the *Guardian*, a stack of Penguin paperbacks secured by twine on her table. Across the room a family — mother, father, lanky teenage daughter — spoke in German. David and Maggie chose a table at the street-side window. The waitress arrived. Maggie ordered orange juice, coffee, a cranberry muffin, a slice of melon. David ordered coffee and oatmeal — "hot cereal" on the menu. When the waitress left to put in the order, David suggested they cancel breakfast and go back to Maggie's room. "I wouldn't hesitate a moment," she said, "except there's a London *Times* cultural reporter coming to rehearsal this morning who I've got to talk with." She looked at her wrist, raising her eyebrows at having forgotten to wear her watch. "I've got to be at the hall by eleven. And where do you have to be, David?"

The waitress set down their breakfasts. She poured coffee for them both. "I have to go to my flat and work on a book proposal," he said.

"Book proposal. For what book?"

David told her about Josef Sudek. His dates: 1896–1976. How he had lost an arm in World War I. How he was closely associated with Prague. How he'd attained fame mainly toward the end of his life. David condensed his knowledge of Sudek in as resonant a summary as possible, wanting Maggie to feel he was capable of wholehearted devotion to an intellectual endeavor. It felt urgently necessary. He didn't know all the reasons why. "I'm really thinking of this project night and day," he said. An exaggeration he desired to be plain fact. "Can I show you some of Sudek's photographs later on? In a book, I mean."

"You know what? I think I've seen a few. In a museum. It may have been here in London. He likes to photograph eggs. Eggs and glasses of water, is that him?"

"That's Sudek."

"I remember an egg with a crust of bread. He might've gone without food some days. In childhood. During the war. Did he?"

"I don't know."

"I guess you haven't researched that part yet."

"I'll definitely look into it."

"Do you take a lot of photographs yourself?"

"Since I was in grade school."

"Are you a professional, though? Along with the teaching you told me about? Not that teaching isn't enough. Just naturally curious."

"I've sold a few photographs. Not often. I consider myself a serious photographer. I have two Nikons. But my favorite is a Rollei — a Rolleiflex with an $f/28$ lens. It's the kind with the viewer on top, you look down into it, like this." He demonstrated by pretending to snap a picture of her. "All three cameras paid for in full at time of purchase."

"So, you take photographs where, London?"

"Mainly Prague. I've been to Prague often. I take a lot of pictures in Prague."

"May I see some of those?" Maggie noticed his hesitation in answering her. With the exception of his Sudek tour, ninety percent of the photographs David took in Prague were of Katrine Novak. "Just to see what the city looks like?"

"Really?"

"Only if you like."

Maggie finished half a piece of toast, drank some orange juice. The waitress stopped by, refilled their coffee. "David, I've got big news," she said. "I'm on an expense account."

"Oh, come on. I'm not the starving-artist type."

"So what if you were? Why should you pay for something neither of us has to pay for? Let Dalhousie University pop for breakfast." Maggie stood up. David remained seated. "I've got to run," she said.

"I'm not taking this for granted. Can I see you tonight?"

"Take for granted? Believe me, I'd see that coming a thousand miles away." The waitress delivered the bill and Maggie signed for it. "The ensemble's performing tonight, eight P.M., Queen Elizabeth Hall. Are you interested? I can arrange a seat directly in front of Miss Brockman and her cello."

"I am interested, but I teach tonight."

"What time is class over with?"

"Ten. Maybe ten-fifteen."

David stood; Maggie leaned down and kissed him lightly. "Let's see, there's the reception. I'm obligated there. This and that. May I expect you in my bed by, oh, say, eleven-thirty?"

"If they'd give me the key, I'd be waiting in your room."

"They won't," she said. "You'll tell me about your class. I'll tell you about the concert."

"Worried there won't be things to talk about?"

Ignoring this, Maggie said, "Tonight's our one concert in London. Noon tomorrow, it's off to Copenhagen. Can you drive me to Heathrow?"

"Of course."

"I don't take it for granted, you know."

"You're so beautiful I can hardly look at you, except I can't help it."

"Temporarily smitten, due to a successful night. No matter; I definitely, *definitely* want to feel beautiful when you say it. But I can't yet. We just met, sort of. Besides, you don't have to say it. I look in mirrors like anyone. I know what I am."

"I could meet you in Copenhagen."

"You don't have a wife, do you?"

"What?"

Maggie looked toward the wide doorway. Five members

of the ensemble were just off the elevator, all casually dressed, holding instrument cases and talking in the hallway. "The cars must have arrived," she said. "I really have to get to rehearsal now."

She joined the musicians in the lobby. In a few moments David meandered into the lobby as well. Looking through the door onto George Street, he saw Maggie get into a black town car. Some of the musicians piled in after her. A cello case was on the front passenger side. The car pulled away from the curb.

David sat in the red leather chair. He noticed that directly opposite, sitting in a kind of velvet love seat, was an elderly, unshaven gentleman. He had on a rumpled gray pinstripe suit, white shirt soiled at the collar, wide gray tie, was sockless with black shoes. He had wispy white hair, age spots on pate and hands, a boutonniere in his lapel and, oddly, a child's zebra-stripe bandage on his left ankle. John Franco stepped in from the street, glanced at the elderly man, exchanged a few sentences in Italian with the concierge, then stood near David's chair. John Franco was a little shorter than David, with thick black hair, sharp features. "That man there cannot meet his expenses," he said.

"What will happen?" David asked.

"I don't know. But first thing, the concierge, Mr. Jimmy Modiano, will somehow find him a pair of socks — maybe maid service found one. Mr. Jimmy always sees the human being. The heart beating. He won't allow a patron of our hotel to go into the manager's office without socks."

"For the dignity of all concerned," David said.

Though it had been John Franco who'd been indiscreet to begin with, now he apparently took offense. It was as if David had presumed to share his approval of a time-honored code of ethics held exclusively between doormen and their concierges. John Franco sneered with his upper lip, all cordiality gone up in smoke. "If that is how you choose to think of it," he said. He walked over and stood next to the concierge. He rigorously cleaned his eyeglasses with a handkerchief, which he tucked back into his uniform's breast pocket in three quick movements, flattening it with a sweep of his thumb. David, as if puppeteered by discomfort, shrugged his shoulders in an exaggerated manner, stretched, faked a yawn. John Franco, with annoyed perplexity, stared at him.

David had simply wished to sit a while longer. To let the life of the lobby quietly go about its business, to be both part of it and an observer of it. Maintaining perhaps the artistic distance of a photographer.

"Can I get you a taxi, sir?" the concierge asked. With this, David relinquished his chair. He walked to his apartment building. His was a nicely appointed flat, with plants along the inside windowsills, lots of books, an antique quilt on the bed, old-style steam radiators, their white paint flaking. David sat on the bed. *Wash your face*, he thought, giving himself instructions on how to kill time. *Maybe go back to the hotel bar — have a cup of coffee — it's okay, stomach feels a lot better, doesn't it? — look directly at that doorman John Franco when you walk past — wait it out — it's just a matter of waiting — it's just a wait of a day and part of a night — it's just a wait until 11:30.*

In class that evening David lectured on a photograph by Sudek, *Bread and Egg*. The photograph depicts a grainy egg set against a piece of bread, which itself is set in relief, offering its sliced side. As the class studied the slide of *Bread and Egg* on the pull-down screen and took notes, David continued to speak, consciously avoiding the term "basic necessities of life," even though bread was involved. He spoke about the photograph within the trajectory of Sudek's thematic obsessions. He also pointed out the sculptural qualities of the composition, how the surface of the crust of bread seemed etched, crosshatched — that is, had what appeared to be an almost geological history.

Though he lectured each semester on Sudek's work, and so already had slides prepared, he originally had planned to discuss a Paris photograph by Brassaï. But *Bread and Egg*, taken in 1950, was the work Maggie had referred to at breakfast, and that was the entire reason for his change of mind; it was a way of keeping her close. After class David sat in the classroom staring at the unfinished letter to Katrine Novak, which he set out on a desk like an important exam he suddenly could not remember studying for. He tore up the letter and dropped its confetti into the wastebasket. *Life*, he thought — indeed, using the word "life," not "circumstances" or "things" — *in just the last twenty-four hours has taken an interesting turn, hasn't it? I'm gone over this woman. I've heard of this happening to other people. I've read of it.*

Their second night together began with heightened anticipation based somewhat on the first. Then they abandoned themselves to even more subtle, and not so subtle, exploration; sometimes in a fugue state of amorous devotion you cannot help what you say; at about 2:30 A.M., David said, "I love your body" (a person might say anything, often something, when memory isolates it from its original context, embarrassing), the most complete sentence possible between breaths. At some other point, Maggie slid herself on top of David and, inside a moan, said, "This feels nice." Then they heard a thud against the wall. They fairly froze; Maggie started laughing; they hung on to each other as if for dear life. David said hoarsely, "Was that a body, do you think?" Maggie's laughter, deep as it was, made things physically a bit awkward, even difficult for David to breathe, the way she lay spent across his chest, her mouth at his ear, her breath softly ratcheting down to normal, almost. Yet they hadn't in the slightest moved apart.

"I believe it was Miss Brockman's cello case," she said.

"Her cello case?"

"She had, or decided she'd had, a bad performance this evening. Haydn's Concerto for Cello and Orchestra in D Major, arranged for the more intimate ensemble. She'll wreck her room. I'll have to smooth things over with management. She'll wreck her room like the Rolling Stones, except all on her own and a bit more demurely. She writes things out on the mirrors in lipstick. Some amazing phrases over the years; she's quite the pornographer. When she gets really worked up. Maid service gets some interesting reading when Miss Brockman's in town and doesn't play well."

David barely began to slip from Maggie; she held him still; David was grateful for this; they'd wait for the next thing to happen. "Do you suppose her cello was in the case?" he said.

"Oh, lord, no. No, no, no. You see, after the concert, I caught a certain familiar look on her face. I told our stage manager, Alistair, to provide the cello safe conduct. He got the empty case back to Miss Brockman's room. Obviously she discovered it empty. That might've set her off."

"And the cello itself is where?"

"Upright in my closet, right here in room 334."

"You know these musicians very well, don't you?"

"Quirky natures, many of them. They each have their superstitions and such, which I find interesting. Onstage they like to be observed. Offstage they can be terribly private, some of them. Miss Brockman's alone a lot, I think. Sometimes I'm her mommy. Sometimes I'm her shrink. Mostly I just get her to the concert on time."

"Okay, three's a crowd. Enough about Miss Brockman."

They turned sideways, facing each other, continued toward a blissful circumstance impossible to resolve by thought; then Maggie said, "At breakfast I had the right to ask about a wife."

"There isn't any wife."

"Because if there is, I'm going to smash Miss Brockman's cello over your head. Because it's covered by insurance. I'll do as much damage as possible."

They listened. Miss Brockman had gone quiet, but Maggie said, "Just wait." Soon they did hear Miss Brockman's muffled voice on the telephone. She alternated sobbing with shouting, silence in between, all of which, had they fully taken it in, might've been a sobering human drama, but they concentrated away from it until it was altogether lost. They fell asleep briefly, waking when the telephone rang on Maggie's side of the bed. "It's her," Maggie said. Five more rings, then the sound of the phone being slammed down. They heard, "Goddammit, Margaret, don't answer, then! What do

I care?" They both moved to the left side of the bed; the sheets were cooler there. They slept again.

"I read a little of your book," David said. It was 7:30 in the morning. He'd already gone out and brought back coffee and cranberry scones. Propping herself against pillows, sheet and blanket pulled up to her neck, Maggie took a sip of coffee, rubbed her front teeth with her forefinger, drank more coffee, took a bite of scone. "Toss me a T-shirt, there, will you?" she said, conscious of having stopped short of adding "darling." David handed her a blue oversize T-shirt, which Maggie slipped on. "This scone is delicious," she said. "Thank you. A very nice way to wake up. I can think of only one better way, but it's too late for that, isn't it?"

David sat in the overstuffed chair. Setting the tray aside, Maggie got out of bed, stepped into the bathroom, shutting the door behind her. In a few moments David heard the toilet flush, the sink faucet turned on and off. Maggie emerged, walked in a comically bent-over fashion, holding the T-shirt stretched down to her thighs, and got back into bed. She took another bite of scone. "So, you read a little Anatole France," she said. *The Crime of Sylvestre Bonnard* was on the bedside table.

"Twenty or so pages is all. Both nights we've spent together, I just opened the book to whatever page and started reading."

"In school, didn't they teach you to start with the first page?"

"Do you remember 'City of Books'?"

Maggie interrupted with an impressive show of memory: "'. . . thereafter made me feel very grateful to Mademoiselle Préfère, who succeeded at last in winning her right to occupy a special corner in the City of Books.'"

"How did you do that?"

"I can recite the odd passage from Proust, too. Some Stendhal. Some Victor Hugo. Maybe five Baudelaire poems in all. But for some reason — maybe I'm a freak of nature — with Anatole France it's like I have a photographic memory. I can't explain it."

"From what you told me, you read him at university till you were blue in the face. I didn't attend university, by the way. Probably you should know that."

"Now I know it. I went to McGill. Junior year in Paris, Collège de France, on an exchange program."

"Why do you read Anatole France in English, then?"

"I speak French pretty well. My reading skills got crummy, and I'm too lazy to work on them. I took half my courses in French. I minored in economics. I guess I thought the combination was 'sophisticated and European,' or something like that. But as it turned out, when I graduated, it was the economics that was useful right away. I got a job working in the business office at Dalhousie."

"How long have you been publicity director, then?"

"Five years. I applied the second I saw the job opening. Want the rest of my résumé, David, our second morning together? First of all, observe this hair. You must have noticed I braid it. Almost every day I braid it. That's from childhood. It's obsessive, but it makes me feel *organized*. I definitely get edgy now and then — you haven't seen this yet. Especially with people who complain about their lives. I cannot stand that. Want to see my nasty dismissive grimace?" Without waiting for an answer, she demonstrated it. Outwardly, it made David laugh; inwardly he hoped and prayed she'd never mean it for him. "I'm too thin, so say some people, my father included. I consider myself homely with a few nice features. My hands have received compliments. My feet have not." Taking this all in, David knew she must've realized by now he found her beautiful. "I'm five feet nine. My nose got broken twice. Ages eight and fourteen, both while ice skating."

They stayed in the room until 8:45. David went to his flat, showered, changed clothes and picked Maggie up in front of the hotel at 10. John Franco placed her suitcase in the back seat of David's rattletrap Citroën, which he'd purchased from his landlord; it needed repairs but they could wait. Maggie said, "I've got a cup of coffee here for you" — then she said it — "darling."

"Thank you," David said. "That was thoughtful." He fit

the paper cup into the holder near the gearshift. Halfway to Heathrow he said, "I can still get a ticket for Copenhagen. I don't teach for a week."

"Better to wait, I think."

The ensemble was at the boarding gate. Maggie led David off to the side, for as much privacy as could be had. "Get everyone else out of your apartment," she said, "launder the towels and sheets, and I'll consider staying with you there a night when I get back, if I want. If you want. I'm keeping my hotel reservation, though, David. At Durrants." She boarded the plane. When she found her seat, she thought, *Did I mean, Better to wait and consider all this carefully? Or did I mean, Better to wait until we can't stand waiting? Or all of the above and more, or what?* On the flight she distracted herself with a "to do" list for Copenhagen.

Letter

IN LONDON, David's apartment was at 813 George
Street. Typing there on his old Underwood manual, he
composed a letter to Katrine Novak; his new devotion
to Maggie was the motivation. He wrote it straight through
in one sitting; he knew if he started to rewrite, there might
be a hundred drafts; it was of course impossible to get it
perfectly right. Still, he and Katrine had a history (quot-
ing Chekhov, she once referred to their relationship as a
"skewed love story"). Fact was, David had seldom visited
Prague without spending at least one night with her. And
while it was true those nights never somehow accumulated
into a declaration of fealty, individually they had allowed for
passion, the value of which, he and Katrine agreed, should

never be underestimated. With the sound of George Street traffic drifting into the kitchen where he typed, David instructed himself to attempt a philosophical intimacy in the letter rather than nostalgia, otherwise it might suggest the possibility of a return to good things. That would be confusing, false encouragement, a lie. No, David needed to close things off.

April 15, 1985

Dear Katrine,

I never thanked you enough for translating the monograph on Josef Sudek — so, thank you, Katrine. That was October of 1982, if I remember right. I need to say goodbye in this letter — because I hope to be married soon. I think, hope, wish to be. The details may be hurtful to you. I don't want that. Suffice it to say I have met someone I feel is the love of my life. I have not known her long. I did not know her during any of our time together in Prague. Though I might sound like I'm trying to absolve myself of guilt, actually I only look forward to the future with her. It would not do you or her justice to not tell you her name — Margaret. There it is, then. I won't be visiting Prague.

While we never, either of us, said "I love you," deep feelings were there, I think. I know on a number of days deep feelings passed between us. This of course is my summary, not yours. I must tell you this is the truth of things. My heart is closed to you. I would expect the same directness from you.

Often in your presence I felt the tremendous desire to sleep after supper. What was that, I wonder? You wanted to stay up in cafés all night. What an interesting life you lead. That must now sound patronizing. Of course it does. But it's true. Your literary friends, your cafés. Your feverish political discussions. I envy it a lot — also sounds patronizing, I suppose. But nonetheless I mean it. Simply, I'm putting all of our time together in perspective. The one thing that unifies every hour walking in the city, every argument, every photograph you let me take of you, everything, was my gratefulness. That might have a hollow ring. I expect it does. I'm sorry if it does.

How to say it? The past has been replaced by the present with Margaret. To quote Anatole France, "Love has its own velocity." (I can hear you just now: "You dare inform me about literature, I'll shoot you in the heart.") Katrine, you are a kind, good, sometimes selfish, mostly generous, very honest, beautiful soul whom I loved as much as I allowed myself to — and let's be honest, as much as you allowed me to. It's never just a matter of doing something "right" or "wrong," is it? You either live steadily with the deeper emotional contingencies or you don't, and to my mind we didn't. Maybe too much distance and absence, London–Prague, who knows? We each had our cities. We both held back but lovely things still took place, didn't they? Both of us tried each other out. In life you just try people out, isn't that how you put it? I'm grateful you tried me out.

David

As soon as he signed his name, David went out to George Street and mailed the letter, in the box situated halfway between his building and Durrants Hotel.

The Veterinarian

THREE-THIRTY A.M., August 7, 1986. David is reading *Manuscript of a Country Doctor*. It is seemingly an endless humid night. Still, David feels a slight chill. The sentence he's just read, "We all step into currents of despair," may have something to do with it. He puts on a moth-eaten, dark blue sweater. Half a peach sits on a plate. The indoor cricket is chirping. The Bach suites for cello are playing.

Not fifty feet from the house a fox — a vixen — loped across the lawn. Head low, tail nearly straight out and wavering, as if batting fox scent toward the swans in order to create panic and confusion in advance of her arrival. The swans came awake. The fox circumvented the pen, driving swans in agitated clusters from one end to the other, whichever was opposite the fox. They stepped and shit right into their wooden water trough. The fox tested the wire mesh with her teeth. In the fog it was as if they were being harangued by a ghost.

Hearing the commotion, David went to the screen door. "What now?" he said.

He kept a rifle in the pantry, a .22 caliber, which had sufficed when a big raccoon somehow got into the pen last winter. He took up the rifle, slid three shells into the chamber and stepped into the yard. He could scarcely make out the pen. David raised the rifle, aimed in the direction of the pond and fired all three rounds. He mainly wanted to scare off the intruder, if in fact there was one. On the third shot he thought he heard a ricochet; possibly he'd hit the metal roof of the bird feeder on its post, and a few seconds later he felt an animal brush past his leg. He looked down to see it was a fox — gone into the fog. Just like that. The fox had actually touched his bare leg, a once-in-a-lifetime thing, he thought, astonished nearly to tears. The swan's Great Enemy had graced David with its stealth and brazen playfulness, the very human being who might have just now killed her.

He felt so grateful, he was tempted, perversely but honestly, to sacrifice a swan to this fox, maybe just loose it in the woods, report it gone missing the next day to William, lying with conviction. Though he'd come to dearly love the swans, he now loved the fox as well. A thoughtless momentum took hold. Exhilarated, he went into the guesthouse, secured the rifle back in the pantry, grabbed a flashlight and hurried to the main house. He woke William up, saying "William, William, William" close to his ear, shaking him by the shoulder. "Wha-a-at?" William said, a bit like a startled goat. "Who the hell's that?"

"It's me, David." David set the flashlight on the bed. The beam mooned out against the wall. (He remembered his own father, Peter Kozol, was good at doing shadow puppets.) "A fox brushed up against my leg, William. I fired three shots at it. Guess you didn't hear."

William had scarcely come into full consciousness. David rattled on about the fox. Finally William said, "Know what I thought first thing when you woke me just now? You almost got me killed in London. You fucking idiot. Not to mention everything else." William turned on his side and went back to sleep.

"Unforgiving son-of-a-bitch," David said. William didn't budge; maybe he had heard, maybe not.

Should not have woken him like that, David thought, walking back to the guesthouse. *In the middle of the night like that.* Should not have expected William to celebrate a miraculous incident. Yet who else was there on the estate to tell? For the first time, at least with such inimitable clarity, it occurred to David that, over the past months, he'd tried to invest any small faith in the possibility not only that Maggie might forgive him — for Katrine Novak, the accident, his dissembling, any or all of it — but that William might consider him part of the family again. Family: he'd addressed this in his notebook. *If only I was back to being part of the Field family* — how inane that read. Yet it was true. *If only William might put in a good word to Maggie for me.* Yet now he was convinced, should he broach the latter subject, William would say, or write: Not till hell freezes over. He would need a second notebook soon.

Stopping a moment on the porch of the guesthouse, David thought, *You fucking idiot.* Or heard the echo of William saying it. It seemed a fitting epitaph: David envisioned it etched on his gravestone. And where would this gravestone be? Not in the Field family plot in Scotland or in the nearby Parrsboro cemetery. No, should he die late that night of an accumulation, slow as an intravenous drip, of poisonous self-pity, corrosive guilt, not to mention desire for his wife, most likely he would be buried in a plot adjacent to one of his parents in Vancouver. He didn't have a Last Will and Testament designating another preference. This little impasse of morbid thought depressed him no end. He felt a crick, a queasy ache in his neck, as if he'd been whiplashed by self-imposed degradation; he felt dumb as a box of rocks, a phrase he'd overheard in the Minas Bakery. Despite being alone, leaning against the screen door's frame, David nonetheless felt embarrassed, realizing that when he'd just now uttered *You fucking idiot*, he'd done so in an imitation of Peter Lorre.

In the kitchen he drank a glass of water, tried to read more of *Manuscript of a Country Doctor*, but his mind kept detouring. He went to the cupboard, took out a bottle of Irish whiskey, poured a shot glass, threw it back. Opened his notebook, scrawled in big sprawling letters YOU FUCKING IDIOT, then went out on the porch carrying the bottle and glass. He sat on the porch swing. Polishing off six shots in less than half an hour, he concluded that the collapse of all good things was due less to grim errors in judgment than to a self-destructive impulse natural to his character. He conjured up probably the most nefarious rationalization possible, in or out of his notebooks: *The sort of thing that happened in London would've happened sooner or later. Therefore Maggie's better off without me.*

Out on the lawn he wandered aimlessly. He had one loafer on; the other was on the porch. It was now well toward dawn. A mile away, lobster boats were on the Bay of Fundy. The lobstermen would see the sun rising. But the pond and surrounding woods of the estate remained socked in with fog. David stumbled to the pen. Leaning against the gate, he said, "Sss-swans, swannies," pathetic now, the alcohol stammer, and then he began calling the swans, "Here, Marcel, here Dr. H," both characters from novels by Anatole

France. For a good two or three minutes, as he repeated the names, the swans didn't react. Finally one trundled over to investigate, got close to David and then, as if a vaudeville cane had hooked its long neck, it effected a U-turn and joined the others near the trough.

David lifted the latch, opened the gate and lay down, blocking the exit. Using outsize movements, like an escape artist loosening chains underwater, he removed his sweater, folded it into a pillow. "I promise I'll go swimming with you, Dr. H," he said, tucking his knees to his chest, closing his eyes. Half a dozen swans folded out from the corner like illustrated Japanese fans come alive. In a few moments David was dead to the world.

Naomi Bloor drove up in her jeep. Her bimonthly examinations were always scheduled for 7 A.M. When Naomi separated a swan out, it most often reacted in a predictable way, a kind of white explosion of wild-eyed protest, until she managed to embrace the swan, chortle "It's okay, it's okay," or hum in a low monotone, then slip the leather hood over its head, at which point the swan generally stilled. She wore a catcher's mask and chest protector, which she'd purchased in a sporting goods store in Truro. It didn't always go smoothly. "Swans, behavior-wise," she told David, "you have to be constantly on the alert. Seeming calm is their best trick. Because it's right then you have to figure some nasty thought's just started to percolate in their swan brains. Wings suddenly flare out. Bony ends of the wings, the bill, both can do real damage." Now and then she asked David to assist. Tasks such as holding a swan's bill closed while Naomi put in eye drops.

On another occasion, Naomi filled David in on how the swans came to be on the estate in the first place. "I get calls from all over this part of the province," she said. "Kids shoot them. A storm caused one to collide with a radio tower, broke its wing. Things like that. Freak accidents. Years back, word got around, the Tecoskys take in wounded swans. I brought them one myself, first year I was the neighborhood vet. You might have noticed one can't turn its neck back to preen? It was shot in the neck's why."

Naomi was thirty-six, with dark blond hair cut in what she called a "serious pageboy." She liked how it framed her narrow face. She typically wore overalls and a cotton shirt and lace-up boots, a utilitarian outfit. While earning her degree at the University of California, Davis, she'd married another student; the marriage didn't last a year. Her first postgraduate posting was with a veterinary clinic in Regina, Saskatchewan. When that ended, she went home to Truro to visit her parents. On this visit she read an ad in a Canadian veterinary journal announcing a "neighborhood practice" for sale in Parrsboro. She inquired by telephone and drove right over. She had lunch, then dinner with Dr. Alvin Frame, seventy-one years old, who'd been born in Yarmouth, Nova Scotia, and had had his Parrsboro practice for forty-seven years. He was tall but stooped, with a head full of white, unruly hair, and Naomi could tell right off he didn't suffer fools. The next morning she drove with Dr. Frame to his office, then to the Tecosky estate. On the way he said, "The caretaker's name is William Field. William, not Bill. I told him we were visiting." Two hours later, while they ate sandwiches at the Minas Bakery, he said, "All right, Dr. Bloor, I'm satisfied you won't reverse all my years of goodwill."

"I hope to extend your goodwill," she said. This made Dr. Frame chuckle, possibly at his own obtuseness.

"Of course you'll do just that. You seem a very competent young woman. You have respectable bona fides. I don't care, really, if this sounds hokey, but my longtime clients, their confidence in me, put two daughters and a son through university. But it's time I get out. Though I won't give up my house in Parrsboro: my wife's buried here. As for the practice, you just study the files, you'll be fine. It's mostly dogs and cats. There's Mrs. Kelb, near Economy, who keeps toucans and parrots, in cathedral cages, you'll see. What else? It's rare but not unheard of the forest service will bring you a deer or coyote someone's hit with a car. I repaired a bobcat once. Like I said, it's all in the files."

"I look forward to the whole thing," Naomi said.

"Well, you can have the whole thing. Including the deep

dark secrets of my accounting methods and tax deductions. You can have my practice lock, stock and barrel, Dr. Bloor." And then he named a price.

Dr. Frame mailed notices of his retirement, which contained a request to welcome Dr. Naomi Bloor. Her first full day at the clinic was diverse, also exhausting. Since she wanted to make a good impression, she spent an inordinate amount of time with each patient and owner. That day, between 7:45 A.M. and 6:15 P.M., she removed porcupine quills from the face and inside the mouth of a mutt who whimpered nonstop, licking the pliers as if pleading directly with them (from 12:30 to 1:00, while she ate a tuna sandwich at the bakery, Dory Elliot told her, "Mrs. Ebbet stopped by, not expressly to say so, but still, she did say you handled yourself well with those porcupine quills. I don't mean to make a pun, but Mrs. Ebbet can be prickly. You got an A-plus on your report card is what I'm saying"); gave regular checkups to three other dogs; put drops of medicinal astringent in the ears of a cat with ear mites. Late in the afternoon a woman from Great Village, Constance Sugrue, called, distraught that her four-year-old daughter, also Constance, used their parakeet's droppings as fingerpaint. "She painted a whole nativity scene on a sheet of manila paper," she said. "I think she inhaled something went to her brain, because why else would she paint a nativity so far from Christmas?" Naomi said, "I don't have a strong background in parakeets,

Constance. I'd call your family doctor. My opinion? I don't think harm was done."

Driving her pickup home to her one-story house in Parrsboro that evening, Naomi stopped to buy a piece of salmon, head of lettuce, tomato, scallions, bottle of olive oil, bottle of vinegar, bottle of white wine. It was a warm night out, a salty breeze off the Bay of Fundy. Listening to the radio, she made oil-and-vinegar dressing, tossed the salad, broiled the salmon. Near dusk she sat on her porch, ate dinner and drank two glasses of wine. Three boys pedaled past on bicycles; they'd each fastened a playing card to the frame with a clothespin and the cards fluttered against the spokes. *I've come into a good situation here*, she thought. *I already know Parrsboro a little bit and like what I know. I'm well past my stupid marriage. Today was a useful day. I'm going to eat my supper and not drink this whole bottle of wine, because I've got an 8 A.M. appointment. It's Mrs. Boomer-Bower's springer spaniel, Berenice.* Mrs. Boomer-Bower told Naomi on the telephone, "My house is on the dirt road off Route 2, just before the cemetery." Naomi wrote this down on a file card.

William had apprised Naomi of the general situation between Maggie and David. ("They're still married on paper," he said.) "I can't think about it much," Naomi said. "I wasn't invited to their wedding, as you know. Still, I wish them the best." However, after David was caretaker for a month, she was flirtatious with him, mostly by indirection. She was scarcely conscious of this at first, then did it on purpose. While examining the swans, she sometimes filled David in on local gossip, talked "out of school" about her women friends' "social lives." She had something of a raunchy sense of humor, though David felt she forced it a little. Dory Elliot called her "high-strung." David found her nice to look at, certainly that; he never confided in her, however, tried never to be anything but civil and direct in her company. He sometimes ran into her at the bakery; they'd had coffee together. He valued her intelligence, her veterinarian's know-how.

Naomi had other designs. Designs that seemed plausible, on the drawing board at least. The previous December she'd asked David to accompany her to a movie in Halifax. He'd said "Sure," followed by "I've been feeling really cooped up here." It was a three-hour drive round-trip, plus the movie itself, so they wouldn't return until quite late. On the drive down they chatted freely. The theater was on Water Street. The movie was *Straight Time*, a psychological character study. Dustin Hoffman played a seedy fellow addicted to robbing jewelry stores; just out of prison, he takes up with a woman who loves him, but when he and another man botch a heist, things quickly go from bad to worse. The woman goes on the lam with Hoffman, but he abandons her at a gas station out in Nowheresville, USA. She asks why she can't go with him. "Because I'm gonna get caught," he says, and drives off.

"Altruism was a phony reason to ditch her," Naomi said in the lobby after the movie. "Though he did do her a favor, didn't he?"

When they stepped out to the street, David's heart leapt, because he thought he glimpsed Maggie walking past. But it wasn't her. "That Dustin Hoffman, as an actor, I mean, he really —"

"Yes, he was very good. But the thing is, I've had girl-friends attracted to men like that," Naomi said.

Late the following January they drove in a minor blizzard to Halifax to see *The Cherry Orchard*, starring Megan Follows, who as a child played Anne of Green Gables on television. Naomi noticed how David looked nervously about the theater as the audience filed in. "I don't see her either," she said. "And I'd understand how you'd be upset if Margaret *was* here." Her saying that had been fine with David. It was the truth.

They left at intermission. Naomi had insisted; she saw it was impossible for David to concentrate on the play. She was put out. "What a waste," she said. "The acting was good." What's more, unbeknownst to David, Naomi had secured a reservation at the Haliburton House Inn, on Morris Street in Halifax. She'd stayed there on two occasions, once alone, once with an attendant at the children's zoo. (She'd mentioned him to David. "When he said he wanted a platonic relationship, I asked didn't he think Plato regularly slept with anyone?") The inn was cozy and discreet, rates were reasonable, breakfast was free with good choices. In the truck, David turned on the ignition, cranked up the heat. Civility had replaced everything; still, Naomi ventured forth. She took his right hand in her left hand and held it against her forehead, as if he should check for a fever. She kissed his palm lightly. David looked out the window. Letting go his hand, Naomi faced stiffly forward. "During the play, I daydreamed us kissing like teenagers — I'll be honest about it. Now I think better of that."

"Look, Naomi —"

"I was just holding hands, David. For comfort, you know? I wasn't suggesting a hotel room."

The next day, from the clinic, she telephoned Haliburton House Inn and apologized for not canceling the reservation.

Naomi noticed David sprawled at the pen's entrance just as she climbed down from her jeep in the driveway. The gate swung back and forth as swans exited. Naomi carried her black veterinarian's bag to the pen. Two swans stepped on and over David's body, one got a solid bite to his nose, and both caught up with three swans along the path to the pond. For all they knew the swanherd was dead. Naomi set her bag on the ground. She stepped over David, kicked at the remaining swans until they, too, set out for the water. She leaned down over David, felt his pulse, decided she didn't need to take out her stethoscope. He had dirty webbed footprints, pasty and dried swan shit and congealed cornmeal on his T-shirt and shorts. The words, in spontaneously antique locution, that came to Naomi's mind were *Behold a pitiful sight.* But pity was not what she actually felt. More, disgust. David groaned awake without opening his eyes. "Guess you're not dead after all," Naomi said. "Well, that's good for you, I suppose." Still, she could not just leave him there. (*Well, I could just leave him here — what harm would come of it?*) She levered up David a little by the shoulders, slapped his face once, patted it roughly. David opened his eyes, said, "My head is pounding." He reeked of whiskey and swan shit. *Quite the unusual combination,* Naomi thought.

"Just drunk as a skunk," she said.

"Where's the swans?"

"The pond. Where else would they be?"

"Any get into barbed wire?"

"What are you talking about?"

Naomi managed to hoist David to his feet. With his arm slung around her shoulder, David leaning heavily into her, too woozy to help much, Naomi maneuvered him in fits and starts to the guesthouse. She kicked open the screen door and with great effort got David into the bedroom. She let him fall face-down on the unmade bed and tilted his head so he could breathe. Naomi went into the kitchen, put on coffee and returned to the bedroom. David was now asleep, snoring like a walrus, but suddenly touched his blood-dried nose, muttering, "Dr. Steenhagen, Dr. Steenhagen." Naomi had no idea whom he referred to, seeing as there was no Dr. Steenhagen in that part of Nova Scotia. She stood there looking at him for a few minutes. She heard the coffee drip. "Oh, what the hell," she finally said. She rolled David onto his back, unbuckled his belt, unbuttoned his shorts, lowered the zipper, slid off the shorts and tossed them into the wicker hamper in the corner, already brimming with rumpled clothes. David wore boxer shorts with a checkerboard design, with black and red checkers on the squares; they'd been a gift from Maggie.

Naomi was about to strip off David's splotched T-shirt when she heard, "You don't mind if I have a cup of coffee, do you? I haven't had one in months." She turned to find William leaning against the doorframe, wearing his robe, pajamas and bedroom slippers.

"I've dragged this poor slob of a son-in-law of yours in here and put him to bed, as you can see," Naomi said. "I probably should have shot him up with something."

"I thought human beings were out of your jurisdiction, Naomi. Professionally speaking."

"Still, I could have put David Kozol here out of his misery."

"Don't do him any favors, eh?"

"I can only imagine how you feel about him, William."

Despite the heat and mugginess, Naomi judged it more seemly to cover David with a blanket, which she did.

"A man who doesn't have the slightest notion of how to handle life," William said. "That's how I feel about him. You didn't rescue him from trying to drown himself in the pond, did you? I wouldn't be able to forgive that."

"He was asleep next to the pen."

"Jesus, no kidding. That's something, isn't it."

"The swans were walking all over him. One by one. Like happy schoolkids stepping over a dead crossing guard."

"Dead-drunk crossing guard, shirking his duties and punished by swans for it. That's got a nice ring to it."

"Yes it does. Well, I've got an appointment in Economy."

"Let's have a cup of coffee together first. It smells good."

"What about Sleeping Beauty there?"

"Let him sleep it off. Other than this pitiful display, I have to admit, Naomi, he's been dedicated to those swans. I have to admit that."

Naomi and William went into the kitchen. Naomi poured two cups of coffee, set them on the table. "Take anything in it?"

"Usually sugar, but I'll pass."

They talked for a few moments. Then William reached out and closed *Manuscript of a Country Doctor*, which David had left on the table. "Laying a book open like that stresses the binding," he said. "My good wife Janice would have protested." He held the bookmark up for Naomi to see. "David Kozol stole this from the library."

"You might better think 'borrowed,' William."

"I'm returning it to its proper place." He slipped the bookmark into the pocket of his robe.

They sat drinking coffee, not talking. Naomi washed out the cups, placing them in the plastic drying rack. "Let's get you back to the house, William," she said.

"There's a morning MovieTime movie on. Some pirate story with William Bendix." He did an imitation of a pirate: "Arr, Arr, Arr, me buckos."

"Not this morning, thanks. I've got that house call."

William's voice was scratchy. "Now *there's* a B actor if there ever was one, William Bendix. He's got that spot in the alphabet all sewed up, you ask me."

"Never heard of William Bendix, I'm afraid."

"It's not important."

William got up from the table. Naomi locked her arm in his. As they started for the screen door, William said, "I thought before I heard David Kozol say 'barbed wire' in his sleep. Could that be right? I don't know why he'd be concerned about that. I cleared every piece of it over a year ago."

"People just say things in sleep."

On the porch Naomi noticed William smiling to himself. "What's so entertaining?" she said.

"Nothing, really. Except, I was recalling a night Janice woke me up. She said I'd said a name in my sleep, but she wouldn't tell me what name, only that she didn't like it. I said don't take it personally. She jumped right on that, though. She felt the opposite, that it's what a husband says in sleep that should be taken most personally of all. Because they can't help who they dream about. And if you don't inform a husband whose name he said in sleep, he can't make excuses. In a way, the wife then owns the secret."

On the grass, they saw dozens of night-woven spider webs beaded and glistening with dew. There were crows by the pond. "Funny thing," William said as they continued toward the main house. "Some mornings I feel like I'm still broken inside. From that taxicab. It's hard to tell the difference between actually being broken and the memory of it."

Daring Nighttime Robbery

MAGGIE MADE three visits in August. That month, too, David took a number of photographs; most were still lifes through rainy windows — so obvious. There were almost daily cloudbursts, lasting only minutes, but otherwise the drought continued. He'd photographed the swans, the elevated black well-cap amongst begonias in the garden, an archipelago of moss on a particularly wide boulder atop the stone wall near the guesthouse. He'd constructed a makeshift darkroom in a small outbuilding. The whole setup — bins, trays, chemicals, paper, enlarger — cost him $1,155. A hose running from the guesthouse provided water. Yet when he appraised the first contact sheets, he recognized the familiar lack of originality, took it harder than expected, threw out the negatives, every last one, stuffed them in the garbage.

Around seven o'clock on the thirtieth, David walked to the pond. He'd allowed the swans to stay on the water, such a disgustingly humid night. He stripped off his shorts, boxer shorts, T-shirt, setting them on the ground, then waded in. The water was slightly brackish from the accumulated heat of June, July and August. He felt the slickness and slope of the hard-packed clay bottom. Up to his chest in water, he stretched out, performed a quick breaststroke, reversed direction, sidestroked back to where he stood again. And that was all, really, he wanted. To gain footing. To hold still. It was a peaceful moment. The slight beaded chill on his skin. The ineluctable strangeness of swimming with swans.

He heard a bass voice originating from the direction of the tree-lined drive leading out to Route 2. It was a car radio; he not only recalled the title, "Duke of Earl," but the singer, Gene Chandler, the Duke of Earl himself. The pulsing refrain, as if Chandler had an amplifier held to his heart as he implored his great love to be his Duchess, the repetition of the word "Duke" two, three, four times in a row at different points in the song, returned with such vivid immediacy that all intervening time between 1962, when the novelty song was popular, and the present was erased. David had always loved that song, "Duke of Earl." When he'd first heard it at age nine, he'd conjectured that the Duke of Earl was an actual figure out of history, and tried to find Earl on a map of England in the big atlas his mother kept in the living room. No luck there.

People lost their way. They sometimes made a wrong turn off the two-lane into the estate. Tourists, visiting relatives of folks in Parrsboro, it might be anyone. At least a dozen times while lying in bed at night, or sitting on the screen porch, he'd heard a car radio. One night he heard a car approach, laughter, then, "Not here, Charlie, can't you see it's private property," then the sound of the car leaving. That had been at 3:30 A.M., the night still young.

The car seemed almost to materialize out of the crepuscular light, crunching gravel under its hubcapped tires, headlights sweeping the main house. David stood ten or so feet from the bank. When the car stopped, he saw it was a 1956 Buick, the exact model and year his family had owned in Vancouver. No doubt he'd heard "Duke of Earl" on the car radio; his mother used to listen to the pop station. "A big stupid American car," she'd say, "but at least I have one. Some divorcées of my acquaintance don't." The mind plays tricks, if it does anything it plays tricks, but this was not the ghost of his father, the ghost of his mother, arrived to Nova Scotia after driving around in the afterlife of Canada all these years. And yet what were the odds of a 1956

Dynaflow suddenly appearing? Seeing as Buick had manufactured thousands of these cars, the conundrum — the uncanny aspect of it here at the estate — was, of course, meaningful only in the context of his own childhood.

The Buick now turned around. *Just someone lost*, David thought. He swam a little — look, the swanherd's hardly a graceful swimmer. The swans kept near the opposite bank. David sidestroked awhile. Then stood again, the water rimming his body, giving him the memory sensation of when he'd stood next to the leather examination couch in Dr. Steenhagen's office, shivering in his skivvies as the doctor held a metal tape measure around his body at chest level. Ardith had brought him in for the swan bite, but Steenhagen decided to add a general checkup, too. He wrote down David's chest measurement, listened to his heart and lungs through the stethoscope, all routine stuff.

"Things look fine," he said to Ardith. "I assure you, this bite is nothing to worry about. No worries here at all. You might expect David to have some soreness, but no infection. It'll heal on its own. Just put the ointment on twice a day as prescribed. Change the bandage. He'll be just fine."

The Buick came back. The headlights were off. David could scarcely make out the car's full definition. Something wrong here.

The car stopped. The driver's-side door opened but didn't

close. The engine idled. David waited, staring at the car. Five or six minutes went by. He then heard a shotgun blast — thundering echo in all directions, it seemed, the pond, the trees, the guesthouse. David saw a figure running from the main house to the car (he hadn't seen it go *to* the house, a trick of light), then heard William's voice, straining but loud and clear, cracking in midsentence: "You broke my window, you cowardly little shit!" William fired off another round; David saw the flash. He heard a branch fall through other branches and hit the ground. William had aimed high on purpose, when he could easily have hit the car. The car door slammed. The car was jammed into gear, wheels spun, the car lurched into reverse, sending up a dust cloud, the spray and hover of gravel dust slightly illuminated when the taillights came on. Then it disappeared.

David witnessed the incident as if it took place in a netherworld of shadow puppets. What snapped him back to his senses was hearing the swans' distress. He turned and saw wings fluttering in the dark, heard wings roiling up water. David scrambled up to dry ground, threw on his shorts, hopping forward the whole time. He ran to the house, yelling, "William, it's me — David! It's me — David!" so as not to be shot.

When he got close to the porch, he stopped, held up his hands as if under arrest, said, "It's me — David."

"Jesus Holy Christ in heaven, will you *please* stop introducing yourself!" William said.

"I was in the pond."

William did not respond right away, but finally said, "Hey, now's an opportunity to knock your lights out, eh? But I guess a shotgun's a bit extreme for that purpose." William laughed hard, coughed a little, cleared his throat. He was wearing a bathrobe and unlaced work boots. He broke open the shotgun, held it slantwise, barrel pointing down and away from David. He stepped off the porch. "Daring nighttime robbery. The little bastard interrupted my favorite opera. Did you get a look at him?"

"No. Too far away."

"I can't tell you how many times I've wanted to take a dip myself, sweltering in my goddamn invalid bed as I was for so long."

"Are you all right, William?"

"I'm the one had the shotgun."

"I didn't even know you owned one."

"Under my bed the whole time."

"No kidding."

"This shotgun was my father's in Scotland. Once in a blue moon I go quail hunting."

"We should call the authorities now."

"The thing is, I know that boy. The hooligan."

"Good, you can identify him. I'll put in the call."

"Oh, hold on a minute," William said. "Hold *on*. Let me tell you something."

"I'm making the call," David said. "It's a Buick Dynaflow he was driving."

"I know the car. I know the boy who drove it. His name is Toby Knox. He's not so bad. He works at the drive-in movie in Truro, or did last I heard, but he's from Parrsboro here. Toby's one of those kids you might first theorize was knocked on the head, maybe playing hockey, and never quite recovered. But you'd be wrong. He's got native intelligence. Though he keeps a good secret of it. Anyway, he's the one broke into the house. What puzzles me, Toby'd likely have known I was in the house, because I'm so seldom *not* in it. Plus, there were a few lights on."

"William, what does it matter? He broke in. A report has to be filed."

"I'm not filing any goddamn report."

William went back into the house; David walked back to the pond. The swans were huddled out of the water. Without visible cue, they stood in unison and, like a weary encampment of white-muslin-clad infantry given marching orders by the wind, moved off along the bank into the cattails, out of view. Yet a few moments later they seemed to pick up the sound of the returning car before David did; the cattails rustled as the swans emerged and bellied out onto the water, their safest haven.

"Alert the Mounties," David said. "The Duke of Earl's back."

He walked to the main house again. The car door opened, a figure stepped out, slammed shut the door. David saw a match flare, caught a glimpse of the young man's face, slicked-back hair, a Hawaiian shirt. The ember of a cigarette like a firefly impaled to the dark. The man took a few steps, then stopped. "I'm the one Mr. Field shot at," he said.

"Toby Knox, I'm telephoning to get you arrested."

"Seems only right."

"It is right."

"Give me a minute to apologize to Mr. Field first. Please."

"You tried to break in and you want me to *let* you in?"

"You're the temporary caretaker, right? David? David, isn't it?"

"That's right."

"Naomi Bloor's my next-door neighbor. See, just now I told you where I live. Mr. Field's known me all my life. I've known Maggie my whole life too. I'm giving myself up."

"Good for you."

David went up on the porch and opened the door and stepped inside. He heard an aria on the phonograph; he didn't know the language. He went to William's room. William lay on the bed with his eyes closed. David knocked on the open door and said, "Toby Knox is outside. He wants to talk with you."

William opened his eyes. "Let him in," he said.

"I'm right here already," Toby said, brushing past David. Toby sat on the end of the bed. "Fuck me, I'm sorry, Mr. Field. Oh, sorry about my language, too."

"Toby, what got into you?"

William switched on the bedside lamp. David got a good clear look at the criminal. Toby Knox was about five feet ten; the word "gaunt" might come first to mind, but that finally best applied to his face, because his arms were solid, biceps stretching the short sleeves of the Hawaiian shirt, with its big blooming white hibiscus on a turquoise background, tucked in. Faded blue jeans, thick belt with a longhorn steer's head on the buckle. His black hair, almost laughably to David's mind, was swept back in a classic "duck's ass." Toby also sported a wisp of a mustache and goatee — halfhearted attempts, more negligence than purpose. He had handsome features. Three times in quick succession, a twitch at the edge of his mouth betrayed his nervousness. He stared at the floor.

"Look at you, Tobias," William said. "The time you spent in London with your cousin last year turned you into a thug of some sort. You used to have a nice look about you. Do you still even admit you're from Parrsboro? You turned into

James Dean. The American movie star who always whined and complained, life's such a bad deal."

"I'm apologizing to you, Mr. Field. Before they take me to jail."

"You like the idea of being dragged off in handcuffs, don't you?" William sighed. "What's playing at the drive-in these days?"

Toby's entire countenance shifted with this change in subject; he straightened right up. "We've got a movie called *Straight Time*," he said. "It was playing in Halifax some months ago, then it ended up on the drive-in circuit. Since the Starlight's the only drive-in in Nova Scotia, we got it."

"What's it about?" William said.

"Basically, it's about a guy who can't stop robbing jewelry stores. He can't seem to help himself. Or, it's more like he helps himself to things he shouldn't, I guess."

"Daring daylight robberies?"

"Both night and day, I think. I can't tell you the whole plot, Mr. Field, beginning to end, because I'm occupied at the concession. I miss a lot of the movie."

"Is that where you got your big idea, Toby, from this movie? The big idea to break into my house?"

"Don't know."

"Difficult to feel inspired from your own resources these days? Your most exciting ideas coming from the movies?"

"I don't know, Mr. Field," Toby said, looking off at the wall.

"I want to see this movie," William said. "If you take me to see it — tonight — now — get me in free of charge, I'll pretend this botched little robbery of yours never took place. Except you'll have to pay for the window you broke."

"You've got a deal, Mr. Field."

"Oh, don't I love a solemn pact," William said, rubbing his hands together gleefully. He looked at the bedside clock. "It's eight twenty-five. We have to factor in the drive to Truro. What time's the movie start?"

"There's coming attractions and such," Toby said. "The movie's supposed to start at nine, but it's usually late. I don't run the projector, though."

"I take it you weren't on concession duty tonight."

"Look, Mr. Field. I'm in over my head with some debts, you know? I wasn't thinking clearly. I was going to grab what I could, try to pawn it down in Halifax."

"Didn't you hear my opera? Didn't you figure me to be home?"

"I thought the record might drown out hearing me. I was only going to take a few items. I didn't even know what. I didn't think it through, Mr. Field. I was just driving by."

"Lame," David said.

"Would you prefer he'd thought about it ahead of time,

David?" William said. "Premeditated robbery of the house of someone's known him since he was born?"

"That's not what I meant," David said.

"Give me five minutes to get ready," William said. "I need to get out of this goddamned house, Toby, so I guess I should thank you for the opportunity."

David and Toby went out onto the porch. There was a vast quilt of moonlight-diffused clouds, no stars. "Use 'Tobias,' all right?" Toby said.

"What?"

"In your report to the Tecoskys. Naomi said every month you send a report to Izzy and Stefania. Saying how everything is. Saying how the swans are doing. What the tree surgeon did, things like that. So I'm asking, when you tell them about my breaking in, refer to me as Tobias, not Toby. They know me as Tobias."

"You fucking idiot."

"I don't care if you tell Izzy and Stefania. I'm just asking you to use Tobias."

William appeared on the porch. He wore threadbare brown corduroy trousers, a blue work shirt, bedroom slippers. "Since I'll stay in the car, I've got slippers on," he said. "Let's go, Toby. I'll sit in back. You're my chauffeur. That car has ashtrays in back, doesn't it?"

"Including on the pull-down armrest in the middle."

"I'm not allowed to smoke. It'll feel good just sitting there in the company of all those ashtrays, though."

"I've got French cigarettes I bought in London," Toby said.

"Don't show them to me."

They walked to the Buick. David called from the porch, "Toby, I don't have to write the Tecoskys — I can telephone them directly. They have telephones over there."

William stopped and beckoned David over. When David stood a few steps away, William said, "The crisis is over. We're going to the moving pictures. The swans are on your watch. I noticed they're still on the pond." William slowly crouched into the back seat and shut the door. Toby got in behind the wheel, revved the engine, let the idle even out, mist swirling in the headlight beams. He gunned it in reverse all the way to the road.

Swans in the House

W HEN THE BUICK'S lights disappeared, David went into the main house to assess the damage. As he passed the kitchen the telephone rang, always a startling thing in an empty house. David stood there through five rings. He felt like the thief. The answering machine recorded Maggie's voice: "Hey, Pop, it's me. Where are you? I'm in my apartment. I had a *day*. Things at work are fine, but I went to the doctor this morning. Guess what? My official due date is November nine. I finally couldn't stand it and had them tell me, so I'm telling you — you've got a granddaughter on her way. And no, don't you tell David, please. When I want to tell him, I will myself. Call me, okay? I want to know you got this news. It's not even nine o'clock but I'm going to bed. Me, the night owl. Love you. Bye-bye."

David thought, *Never mind the due date — no one told me Maggie was pregnant to begin with!* He went to the guesthouse, circled November 9 on the calendar, sat drinking coffee, thinking back to the night he and Maggie had last slept together, February 10.

Though it seemed impossible, the fact was, between the accident in London and February 10 of this year, he and Maggie had not met each other's eyes, let alone had any sort of conversation. Nor *since* February 10, for that matter. From his kitchen window, David occasionally glimpsed her driving up to or away from the estate, or strolling with William to the pond and back. Now and then he'd impulsively telephoned Maggie's office, and her assistant, Carol Emery, would say, "They're in France," or "They're in New York," or even "They're in town," but he had the distinct feeling she'd been instructed to keep such information to a minimum.

Early on the morning of February 10, Maggie drove to the estate, stayed late, and while driving back to Halifax she stopped at the all-night diner for a cup of coffee. There was blowing sleet. Maggie had the windshield wipers going. In the parking lot, before turning off the ignition, she saw David through the diner window. He was paying his bill at the cash register. She sat there, heat cranked up, watching her husband complete his transaction. Neither the car's nor the diner's window qualified as amorous, that was for certain. You can't help where your mind goes, however; Maggie felt the pitch and seethe, the opposing forces of love and hate, though there was a unifying element: she still felt David to be the love of her life. (At the same time, she thought, *He has not come to Halifax to say that very thing about me, has he?*) This surprised and saddened her, and then she experienced a surge of disappointment in herself for feeling it. That is, her emotions ran the gamut.

David stepped from the diner, his breath ghosting out — *Put on your gloves,* she thought. He noticed her car and stopped abruptly, watching Maggie appear and disappear behind the streaking sleet as the wipers arced back and forth. The parking lot had patches of black ice. He walked, slipping once, catching his balance, to her car. Maggie didn't roll down the window. They looked at each other a moment, then David walked to his truck and climbed in. He fully expected Maggie to continue on to Halifax, but in the rearview mirror saw that she was following him to the estate.

Once inside the guesthouse, Maggie took off her coat and said, "David, I really don't want to talk. I can't bear it." She stood next to the bathtub and dried her hair from the sleet.

Viewing this from the kitchen, David felt so grateful for her presence — the painful familiarity in the way she bent slightly, let her hair fall, rubbed it with the towel in furious eddies — that it unhinged him a little. He sat down at the table, his coat still on.

Finally he followed her into the bedroom.

She left at 1:30 in the morning. "I'm driving straight back to Halifax," she said. "I'm going now, David." On the return drive she stopped and got that cup of coffee. As she sat sipping it in a booth, her heart felt scored by anger and blame. Nonetheless, she came up with a pairing of words to help her get purchase on the fact of having just slept with her estranged husband: "necessary and confusing" (once she learned she was pregnant, she revised this to "necessary and nostalgic"). She felt a slight cold coming on.

When Maggie got to her apartment on Robie Street, she took a bath, sat in her robe listening to the BBC on her broadband radio, a gift from her father, for almost two hours, trying not to think. She dressed in a favorite pair of black slacks, a peach-colored blouse with a button-down black sweater and, for the first time since her honeymoon, the simple pearl necklace David had given her in his London flat, for what he called their "one-hundred-day anniversary." It began to snow. Putting on her overcoat, gloves and galoshes, carrying a pair of shoes in an oversize handbag, she left for her Dalhousie office; there was paperwork to catch up on before a 9:15 appointment.

If love has its own velocity, so does love in absentia. He put on a clean T-shirt. He should have taken a shot of whiskey and tried to sleep, or read Anatole France, or listened to Bach. What was that phrase Maggie's mother used when Maggie was anxious about this or that? *Be patient, life will provide.* David wasn't so sure. However, he opted for none of the tried-and-true routines of the past year. Instead, he committed himself to a sequence of actions, each one by itself so compulsive, reckless, he didn't fear or probably detect their cumulative destructive effect. *How could I do more harm than I've already done?* he might have reasoned, if he reasoned at all. Whereas he should've just called it a night.

First he walked to the pond and saw the swans gathered on the far bank. He approached, then dropped to his knees, crawled close, reached under the nearest swan's backside and attempted to lever it into some sort of reaction — it swung around and bit his shoulder. A significant jolt of pain made him recoil, but he recovered quickly, crawled again toward the gather of now pissed-off swans, all still hunkered down. David let loose a kind of seal-barking: *Arrk, arrk, arrk.* One swan flared its wings, and in a hydraulic motion raised up and settled down, then waddled off a short ways. Almost immediately there ensued a domino effect: the swans lined up, went single file to the path, began down it toward the pen. However, when they got within feet of the pen David caught up; he began to shout and administer kicks, herding the swans toward the guesthouse. They bustled up onto the porch, crowding at the screen door, so that David had to struggle to get it open.

The swans clambered in, and for some reason the lead swan was almost magnetically drawn to the open-topped plastic garbage pail in the cabinet under the kitchen sink, whose hinged door David had left open. It stretched forward, and in an instant attacked the garbage. The pail was so full that a filter of wet coffee grounds floated at the rim. The swan submerged its head, came up for air and, having nabbed the filter, scattered grounds with a wild shake of its head. A second, then third swan followed suit, tearing into the garbage, which held peach pits, grapefruit rinds, banana peels and apple cores, then abandoned it. Meanwhile, in the sitting room, half a dozen swans went haywire, possibly reacting to having seen their reflection in the oval, full-length mirror in its wood frame on the back of the half-closed bedroom door. Or maybe they'd responded to the Van Morrison record on the turntable, a voice without visible source.

In something of a panic now, David chased the swans with a broom like a cartoon witch, shouting, "Get out! Get out!" Which sounded stupid even to him. Besides, when you invite guests in, you should show them a good time. In the sitting room, yet another swan knocked over a tall vase containing dried cattail rushes, which smashed against the cobble fireplace. It then got a leg caught in the cord connecting the phonograph to the wall socket; immediately the Van Morrison tune "Tupelo Honey" became a horrible scratch as the turntable was yanked to the floor. At which point the swan started biting the vinyl record. The phonograph's arm was twisted upward, the swan stepped on the needle and lurched, snapping at its own foot as if bitten by a serpent.

David hurried to the pantry, took up the .22 rifle, shoved in a few rounds, fired three shots into the sitting room over the heads of the swans wreaking havoc. One bullet webbed a crack in a window, another splintered the headrest of a rocking chair, a third neatly entered the wall near the fireplace. The swans sat down. David set the rifle on the kitchen table, said, "I've done some real damage here," a statement that stood for so much. He picked up a peach from the bowl, took a bite of it, spit it out, the most familiar and pleasurable taste in the world to him somehow rancid, though it was a perfectly good peach. He glared at the swans. Half of them squatted there in the sitting room, the rest were in the kitchen. They were mute and some had actually begun preening. One swan sauntered over to the fireplace and sat on the empty grate like an iron nest. "You have ugly natures," David said.

He stood up, put his mouth to the spigot in the kitchen sink, turned on the faucet and drank with loud gulping. It was as if the well water was laced with adrenaline, because David began shouting, "I have got to get out of here! I have got to get out of here!" about thirty times in a row, in a repetitive tone like a skipping record.

David now turned to the novels of Anatole France. He slid the stack from the counter, clutching the books against his chest. Securing them at the base with his belt buckle, at the top with his chin, he kicked open the screen door. Leaving the guesthouse to the swans, he carried the books down and dropped them near the pond. Then he flung each one in the manner of skipping stones. Water immediately saturated *Patroologica* (it was the book most in disrepair, frayed spine, pages taped, though probably it was the angle at which it hit the water that caused it to sink so quickly). The rest landed and floated, covers facing up or down, like illustrated lily pads. A few soon sank, others drifted, indicating a slight current or breeze.

David choked back three or four sobs in quick succession, countering with a kind of hyena laugh, shouted over the pond, "So fucking *hot* out!" as if that was the cause of all this madness. Easiest to blame what could least be helped. He again slipped out of his shorts and T-shirt, both of which he balled up and tossed aside. Lying naked on the grass, he closed his eyes. Sounds drifted down from the guesthouse. "Oh, Jesus, I think they've got into the cupboard," he said. "Daring nighttime robbery. Perpetrated by swans."

He dozed off in the sticky heat, but in half an hour woke to music from a car radio approaching down the drive. Toby Knox's Buick stopped at the main house. Toby switched off the ignition. He and William were talking, but David couldn't make out the words. And then William suddenly raised his voice: "Holy Mother, Jesus and Mary!" Searching frantically for thirty seconds or so, David found his shorts and shirt, put them on and walked up the slope. William and Toby were already heading to the guesthouse to investigate. They all met up on the porch.

William looked through the open screen door. He turned and said, "Toby, it appears that the Tecoskys' swans are inside a house."

"That's not good, Mr. Field," Toby said.

"I can explain," David said.

"Did you invite them in for tea?" William asked. He stepped forward and clocked David a solid right to the jaw. David careened back onto his butt and sat there, too stunned to reach for his jaw or try to utter a word. The arc of the punch had thrown William off balance too, and Toby had to catch him. "Whoa, there, Mr. Field," Toby said, helping William regain his footing.

"I felt something crack, and it wasn't in my hand, either," William said. "David, you might want Toby here to drive you to the hospital for an x-ray."

David shook his head no. His jaw throbbed; without touching it, he felt it swelling.

"Okay, then, I've finally knocked my son-in-law's lights out, like I've been promising for over a year. So it can't come as a surprise to him. I'm going in and put some ice on my hand and go to bed. Toby, don't fashion yourself after that lowlife played by Dustin Hoffman, eh? It's your life, Tobias. But you break into my house again, I'll shoot out the windows of your car with my shotgun and only half hope you're not in the driver's seat."

"I've figured that all out already, Mr. Field," Toby said. "You ever want to go to the Starlight again, just ask me. I'll personally drive you there."

"Don't forget you owe for the window."

David wiped blood from the corner of his mouth. He made a sucking sound, felt pain travel up to his left ear. Oddly, his neck and shoulders hurt too, as if he'd been completely realigned. He slurred, "Hope you're happy now, William. You broke my jaw, I think." It had been like trying to talk after the dentist shot you up with Novocain, your mouth stuffed with cotton and clamps, except the pain was still there.

"I'll expect the swans to be out of this house promptly,"

William said. "You can get them out, broken jaw or no. Rise to the occasion, David. I'll probably be docking your paycheck to cover getting the rug cleaned. I noticed a broken vase, too, and that was just from a quick glance. First thing in the morning I'll call Stefania and Izzy over in Scotland and tell them there's been a change of guard, that I'm back as caretaker of their estate. I bet they might let you stay on as my hired hand, though. In fact, I'll make that recommendation, gentleman that I am. A man needs employment."

David merely stared at William. He heard the swans marauding through the kitchen. Looking at David, Toby said, "I'm officially offering to help you clean up in there. Five dollars an hour sound all right?"

"Don't ask him," William said, "ask me. You're hired."

William walked back to the main house. David grasped the porch railing and tried hoisting himself up, but fell back. He was dizzy, his eyesight blurred. "The hospital in Truro's just over half an hour. You get me driving at my best," Toby said. "Anyway, you look like shit."

Toby offered his hand. David swept it away violently. Toby said, "Come on, David, don't act like you haven't just been knocked on your ass by an old man."

"He was an amateur boxer in Edinburgh," David said, the word "Edinburgh" sounding like "Essdingburk" through his lacerated tongue and swollen jaw. He suddenly felt parched. Toby again offered a hand up; this time David accepted.

Toby pulled him to his feet. "Need a minute," David said, leaning against the house.

It took about forty-five minutes to get the swans gathered on the porch. "They're bigger than I thought, close up like that," Toby said. Jaw pulsing the whole left side of his face, David went into the bathroom, opened the cabinet, took out a bottle of aspirin and swallowed three tablets, cupping water to his mouth from the spigot after each one. He examined his face in the mirror — a bit of a shock there. He dabbed Mercurochrome on the knuckle-gash near his mouth. When he returned to the porch, he saw that Toby had already herded the swans into their pen. Toby latched the gate and walked back, and when he stepped onto the porch, David said, "Hospital."

At nine o'clock the following morning, William visited David in room 311 of Truro General Hospital. Visiting hours hadn't officially begun, but William presented himself as "family" at the information desk. David shared a room with a telephone worker who'd had an emergency appendectomy. There was a curtain drawn between their beds. David sat up straighter against the pillows when William entered. His jaw was wired shut, the left side of his face bruised predictably black-and-blue, plus his chin had summoned up a yellow splotch with a black outline, like a watercolor painting. First thing, William said, "I called Maggie and told her you're in the hospital. She asked how bad it was, and I told her my opinion. She said she's not going to visit, but that I should say get well soon. To my mind, that's somewhere between nothing and something, which you might consider an improvement in your relations, I don't know."

David nodded, smiling wanly, but remained silent.

"My daughter doesn't need me to fight her battles. This was my own battle, between me and you, for the taxi hitting me. Just so we get that straight. Margaret didn't approve of my actions."

David touched the bruised side of his face, pressed the buzzer at the end of a white cord, hoping the nurse would release more morphine into the IV. In a moment a nurse poked her head around the curtain. "Nurses' station said you had a visitor," she said. "How nice."

"Painkiller," David said, but it came out "fain kiffper." The nurse had heard it pronounced any number of ways. She was in her early fifties. Her name was Kristin Fournier.

"I understand you're related," she said to William.

"Father-in-law," William said.

"Your son-in-law here's asking for an anodyne."

David didn't know what the word meant, but William said, "Who doesn't need that, eh?"

"There's all sorts, of course," nurse Fournier said. "I get

mine from church. But Mr. Kozol needs one through the drip. I've been a nurse half my life. I can read his expression."

She studied the chart on a clipboard tied with string to the bed frame. She fluffed up David's pillows, gently inspected his mouth and jaw, refilled the plastic water cup on the adjustable tray, replaced the straw. "Be brave, Mr. Kozol," she said. "You have an hour's wait. It's a good hospital that keeps track of such things."

When the nurse left, David looked at William, and only then did he notice that William was somewhat formally dressed, herringbone sports jacket, corduroy trousers, dark shirt and tie, clothes far too heavy for summer, especially this one. David took up a pad of paper and wrote on it, tore off the sheet and handed it to William: *Can you sneak a whiskey in here for me?*

"Oh, I don't think that particular anodyne's allowed."

David closed his eyes.

"The estate's back in good hands now," William said. "Don't fret over the swans, for example. Don't concern yourself one bit."

David mumbled something incoherently.

"Hard to understand you," William said. "I know what that's like, don't I, having to speak through all that pain and pills. I'm scarcely just past it myself."

David — for the first time — said, "I'm sorry."

"By the way, feel free to stay on in the guest cottage. I've spoken with Izzy and Stefania. I'll nurse you back to health. The doctor will no doubt recommend soups. I'm an expert at soups, don't know if Maggie mentioned. I made soup for her every winter day, elementary school." William pulled up a chair and sat. "I've got an idea. What if tomorrow I bring in the photograph albums from Maggie's upbringing? Janice was absolutely devoted to those albums, my lord. I keep them in a fireproof safe. Anyway, it might be a useful education. You might get to know better who you're married to."

"I'll provide the commentary," William said at ten the next morning. He'd brought three photograph albums. He was dressed in exactly the same clothes as the day before, no tie this time. He set the albums on the bed. He took off his sports jacket and put it on the back of the chair, which he pulled close to the bed. He opened the first album across David's lap. "This one takes Margaret up to age twelve."

David wanted to say, "I'm going to take a lot of photographs of our daughter," but held back. First, it was difficult for him to speak at all, though he could've written it out. Also, it wasn't the right time to reveal that he knew Maggie was to give birth in November. William was keeping the news to himself; he'd brought the albums to bring David up to speed on Maggie's childhood — things should go in the proper order.

Each photograph was held to its page with black adhesive triangles at its corners. (*My mother's company manufactured these*, David thought.) "Going left to right," William said, "this is Maggie's first bath. In the kitchen sink, believe it or not. This next one's me holding her, then there's Janice holding her."

David pointed to a photograph of another woman bathing Maggie and got a quizzical expression on his face. According to the date written underneath, Maggie was three. "Oh, boy," William said, "that's a much younger Dory Elliot. She was Janice's dearest friend. For a while there. Back then the word 'pretty' wouldn't've done her justice, believe me. A lot of men drove great distances just to order a scone at her bakery. You won't find Dory in any history book, but she's got a history. She's done a lot more than make thousands of lemon tarts and her famous coffee cake in her sixty-one years. For instance, did you ever look at those framed newspaper articles behind her counter? I know you go into the bakery a lot. Next time, look at them. It's Dory, late teenage years and early into her twenties. She entered a number of Canada-wide beauty pageants and sometimes won. I mean first place. What's more, Dory was a gifted lifeguard. Saved a boy's life in front of his family, that was near Peggy's Cove. She was married and divorced twice, started the bakery and stayed that course. Her hair, you've noticed, is completely white, but that happened at around forty, not later. Happened almost overnight; she was in the hospital with a heart infection. As I mentioned, she was Janice's dearest friend for many years. But that's another story altogether."

After the nurse replenished the morphine, David ate a few bites of Jell-O, sipped some ice water, chewed on ice chips as William finished with the album, all black-and-whites: Maggie's first day of school; Maggie putting on lipstick, Janice putting on lipstick beside her; Maggie and William in a rowboat on the pond; Maggie in pajamas, a thermometer in her mouth, Janice worriedly looking on, but so exaggeratedly that David could tell she wasn't truly worried.

On the next-to-last page was a photograph that showed Maggie sitting with Isador and Stefania on the porch steps. "Now, this was an unusual conversation they were having," William said. "About as unusual as can be imagined. Maggie's ten there. 'Why do you have those numbers on your arms?' — that's what she asked. She started crying before she heard the answer; must've felt bad news in advance. Stefania didn't go into the details. Too painful to tell, too painful to hear told. But she did introduce the words 'concentration camp,' didn't hold back there. Believe me, Maggie could be very direct, very curious. 'There were people called Nazis. They tried to kill all the people of our religion, Jewish people, but we're here, aren't we?' That was the history lesson that morning, except Maggie didn't let it go, even when Izzy added, 'That was over in Europe before you were born.' I can't put the full psychological whys and wherefores to it, but they sat there a good two hours. And if you think I'm being sentimental, guess again, because Maggie had nightmares, oh, I'd say six, seven nights running. Into Janice's and my bed, hopped right in between us, pulled the blanket over her head. One night she said, 'I looked in on Izzy and Stefania, and they're fine. You check on them later.'"

William put on his sports jacket and went to the hospital cafeteria for lunch; David slept an hour. When he woke, William was sitting in the chair, staring at a page of photographs in the second album. David chewed on some more ice chips. William set the open album on the bed, leaned close and said, "Now here's 1968 to 1972 — the Vietnam War raging, huh?"

But David had written a note, which he handed to William: *You really went on about Dory Elliot, I must say. I've been wondering why she hasn't once been to visit you. Not once.*

William tightened his mouth, closed his eyes a moment, opened them, moved the chair back a little, absent-mindedly buttoned his sports jacket. "I did go on about her, didn't I," he said. "Look, David — now that you're a captive audience. Now that things have come around like they have. We keep getting thrown together, eh?"

David wrote another note: *There's no taxi in here. You aren't going to punch me again. Just say it.*

"There's nineteen swans on the estate now, correct?" William said. "Well, when Maggie was seventeen, there were twenty-eight. It was a regular lying-in hospital for swans that year. Anyway, and these lines are wide enough to read between, David. Very wide. For a short while I took up with Dory Elliot. Then it ended. And this was Janice's dearest friend — though how could she have been, to partake of something like that? Maggie'd be in the bakery practically every day after school. I think she confided more in Dory than in Janice, for a stretch, but that's the way it goes, mother-daughter, sometimes. Just normal. In any event, Maggie and Janice ended up very, very close. I was always grateful for that.

"But Dory — it was a cruel thing to do, though she's not cruel. Told Maggie the whole sordid thing. Maggie drove home and confronted me. Then she told Janice. Then she packed a suitcase for herself and one for Janice. They drove to Halifax and stayed for five nights. Janice continued on to visit her sister in Edinburgh for a month. When she came back it was the ice age in my house for a long time. Eventually things were workable. But once trust gets dropped — and I dropped Janice's like an anvil from — what floor was your London hotel room on? From the fourth floor of a hotel. And I never entirely got it back. Mostly, but not completely."

They sat awhile; David fell asleep without meaning to,

just nodded off despite the moment; William thought it was a reprieve. Finally William woke him up. "Lately I've given things a lot of thought. Take it or leave it. It's not meant as advice, just observation. But it occurred to me, in reliving what I put Maggie through with my dallying, that it might just be one reason Maggie's so — *unforgiving*. Mind you, I said *one* reason. I mean, connect the dots, David. Whatever you did or didn't do in that hotel room wasn't the same stupidity, but it had certain approximations."

David wrote another note: *That couldn't have been easy to say. But you've worn me out.*

Without another word, William took up the albums and left the room. But he telephoned David from the lobby. David managed, "William," because who else would it be?

"I don't feel I'm wasting my loose change here," William said. "The thing is, young couples, when they're courting, they have to feel like they're inventing happiness, eh? Inventing it. Because they're supposed to feel that. They can't help it. Nothing new in this.

"As far as I could tell, you and Margaret had what I'd call a whirlwind courtship. All through she kept calling me, keeping me apprised, to the extent she chose to. I mean, how you flew back and forth, Halifax–London, London–Halifax. Maggie almost used up her savings, did you know that? 'I'm spending the weekend in London, Pop,' was not the prudent Margaret I knew. Prudent of heart and prudent of purse is a world of difference. Even a protective father understands that fact of life. I was following her the way that dotted line in the old wartime movies showed a ship or airplane crossing the Atlantic Ocean. I knew Margaret was head over heels. And how that boosted my spirits on her behalf.

"I'm not going to predict the future. Whoever's in the prediction business is a damned fool. But as for the past, I like to think of you and my daughter inventing happiness. But then along comes that London hotel room. What was I supposed to do, David, *not* tell my own daughter what I saw? Did you think it was a separate moral universe or something, a hotel room? Anyway, for your information, with Margaret I didn't speculate past sheer description, just that I saw a woman standing in her bathrobe. Obviously that was enough to set things in motion. I knew it. No matter what the whole truth was. The day after your honeymoon, lord in heaven."

William listened a moment; with every possible effort, David managed, "I know our daughter's due on November ninth." They both hung up.

In his hospital bed, David wondered if pain might sharpen his comprehension of what William had said. To that effect, he considered refusing the next round of morphine. Besides, if he felt competent at anything, it was sleepless nights. He was an expert, one might say.

Wedding in Nova Scotia
(1985)

O
N JULY 27, Maggie arrived at the estate at 7:30 in the morning. She sat with William at the kitchen table. He'd prepared hot cocoa. William wore his pajamas, robe, slippers. Maggie had on gym shorts, a sepia T-shirt under a white cotton blouse, no shoes. "You didn't drive without shoes on, did you?" William said.

"I often do, in the summer."

They spoke about things in general. Then Maggie said, "David's proposed marriage."

"No fool, is he? Have you decided when's the wedding?"

"We were thinking in ten days."

"Ten days?"

"I've already called everyone we want invited. They're all available. That's good luck from the get-go, I'd say. David has no family. I've told you, his mother and father are gone. Buried in Vancouver. He's got no family but you and me."

"Who's going to stand up for him?"

"He is."

"And for you?"

"Frannie Dunsmore."

"Your closest friend since when, sixth form or so? It'll be good to see her again. In ten days."

"I know it's short notice. But it'll be an informal wedding. I asked Dory to make the wedding cake. Just so you know."

"Of course she's not invited to the ceremony."

"Would I do that?"

"All right, then, a lot can get done in ten days."

"Some of the ensemble's agreed to play."

"How about that?"

"Anne Stevenson at the Glooskap said she'd arrange for food."

"You can't go wrong with Anne Stevenson and food. She'll provide a feast. Possibly some surprises, too. Like the time she put cherry vodka in a summer soup. You might request that."

"Wait here, Pop. I'll be back in a minute."

Maggie went upstairs, and when she returned she was wearing a Victorian-era white dress with a lace collar and hem.

"Your mother's wedding dress seems to fit," William said.

"Dad, you forgot to take the dry-cleaning tag off. Maybe you forgot on purpose, huh? Interesting, after all this time you suddenly get it in your head to have this dress cleaned in Truro."

"I had an inkling."

"An inkling to you is absolute fact for anyone else."

"Who's performing the ceremony?"

"I thought Robert Teachout."

"Reverend Teachout? I thought he was long retired."

"He's not retired. People just don't give him work anymore. He moved to Advocate Harbor."

"You've done all your homework already. A bit skulking under the dark of night, though, don't you think? Why couldn't I know this big secret till now?"

"David proposed to me night before last."

"Margaret, you've done things your own way since I can remember." He took a sip of cocoa. "He didn't get down on his knees, did he? He's not a dramatic personage, is he?"

"As a matter of fact, no. He asked like a gentleman, not copied out of a book or movie. It was a genuine marriage proposal carried out in a thoughtful manner."

"So I'm finally going to meet your David."

"He's at the pond."

"I'll go down there."

"Let him come here, Pop. I'll get him."

"We'll have ten days to get to know each other, then. That's one hundred percent longer than no time at all."

"Did you hope he'd ask for my hand in marriage?"

"Yes."

"Please don't start by testing his good breeding. He didn't have a father at home much at all. He came to a lot of his knowledge of how to act on his own."

"You asked, I answered, that's all. He doesn't need defending. Bring him up to the house. I'll put on some more cocoa."

They had every meal together after that. Maggie attended to wedding arrangements. She took David around to meet Dory Elliot when the cake was discussed. Midmorning on August 1, William went to the guesthouse to get David. On the way, he saw David looking at the swans. They both stood there a moment, then William said, "Our veterinarian says these wing-clipped swans keep forgetting they can't fly. The urge to fly is a million years older than their wound, so they forget. Now, that's a sight — a swan who can't fly. It's as comical and heartbreaking as Buster Keaton trying to catch a bus."

David laughed hard, trying to picture it. "Come on up to the house," William said. "I've got something to show you."

Maggie, David and William sat at the table. Letters were stacked up, all handwritten on official-looking stationery. "These are letters I've received from a very admirable man," William said. He was addressing David. Maggie knew all about the letters. "His name is Reginald Aston. Mr. Aston is no less than the Queen of England's official swankeeper. In the greater London area alone — and I might have these statistics wrong — Mr. Aston has over two thousand swans under his jurisdiction. Naturally the population shifts — boating accidents, natural deaths."

"Tell David about the kidnapping, Pop."

"Two thugs kidnapped a swan along the Thames. It was witnessed by passersby, yet the crime remained unsolved. Why someone would do that beats me. You lived in London, David. Any swan you saw was in Mr. Aston's keep."

"My dad has something to ask us," Maggie said, knowing if she didn't get to the point, William might read Mr. Aston's letters out loud and David would be too polite to say anything.

"Right. Well, I've got an appointment with Mr. Aston, long-sought. It's on August nineteenth at noon. Maggie tells me you're flying Halifax to Boston, then on to London, on August sixth. I thought I might get a seat on the same airplane, see London as a tourist while you two go off to Islay. I'd visit the sights. I'd meet my August nineteenth meeting with Mr. Aston. I might even stay on another week."

"What was the concern, William?" David asked.

"You might not want a father-in-law along, the start of a honeymoon."

"Maggie has to fly back to work in Halifax when our ten days on Islay are over," David said. "I have loose ends to take care of. I've already closed down my flat, but I have to close my bank account. Things like that. So, if you are staying in London, maybe we could have dinner. Or just take a walk in one of the parks. I might suggest Regent's Park."

"From the look on your face, Margaret, I see you're in agreement."

"There, now that's over with," Maggie said. "Let's take a swim."

"You two go on," William said. "I swam at five this morning."

The wedding took place on the lawn at 4 P.M. There was a merciful breeze. The swans were on the pond. The ceremony was brief. Three musicians from the Dalhousie Ensemble, including Marianne Brockman, played pieces Maggie had chosen: selections from Bach, Haydn, Antonio Caldara. There were twenty-three people in all. Toby Knox represented Parrsboro. Frannie Dunsmore came down from

St. John's, Newfoundland, with her husband, Duncan Mc-Gary, and their daughters, Mary and Ileene. The lemon wedding cake was a three-tiered architectural wonder. Dory had asked Ezra Murry, a mechanic and woodcarver, to whittle a bride and groom; he could expertly paint on a gown and tuxedo, plus the faces. Ezra replied that he could easily carve a likeness of Maggie as a bride, but declined the request, since he'd never met David. Dory got this message to Maggie, who drove David to Ezra's house in Lower Economy, where Ezra got a good look at him. Maggie and David stayed fifteen minutes. The wooden bride and groom turned out splendidly. David had picked up the cake; he and William carried it in from Maggie's car as if delivering high explosives, set it on the kitchen counter.

William borrowed a French country table, which he set parallel to the one already in the dining room. Maggie set out the Tecoskys' best china and silverware. She had asked permission by phone, after inviting them to the wedding. "We'd love to be there," Stefania said, "but we're not up to traveling just now." Maggie and David washed every spoon, fork, knife, wine glass, plate.

An hour after the ceremony, the meal was served. The ensemble's musicians played. William gave a toast, which he'd written out: "I'm as proud and happy as can be to see this marriage take place." That was it; he held up his glass and everyone at the tables held up theirs. When dishes were cleared, out came the cake. David took ten photographs of it. Marianne Brockman took a photograph of Maggie and David cutting the cake.

Off at the far end of the living room, Reverend Teachout remarked, "They make a nice couple, don't they? From opposite sides of Canada, isn't that something? Course, they rehearsed their wedding night months before the wedding. But a lot of young people do these days, don't they? I've heard some even rehearse their wedding night and don't eventually get married. Margaret and David, there, had wedding vows almost shorter than the kiss that sealed the promise." He seemed to marvel at how passion sometimes abbreviates what precedes it, in this case his few platitudes about life and love, though quite well spoken, everyone thought. "Ah, well," he said taking a bite of cake, "I have officiated at hundreds of weddings, and I always think it redundant to say 'You may now kiss the bride.' Because the groom in question doesn't usually *need* to be instructed so. Bride neither."

The guests all left by ten o'clock. The musicians had arrived in two separate cars from Halifax. Marianne Brockman, who had drunk a lot of champagne, told Maggie and David she thought she'd played quite well, especially the Haydn; Maggie and David cracked up, remembering their night hearing Miss Brockman through the wall of their hotel room. Miss Brockman had to be assisted to the car by the other members of the ensemble. She was placed in the back seat, her cello in the front seat.

Maggie and David spent their wedding night in the guest-house. William set two new fans in the bedroom; they were already on. "Thoughtful of William," David said as Maggie and he were stepping out of their wedding clothes.

"And knowing —" she said.

"It's all right. It's fine. Besides" — they were kissing deeply — "the need right now is, don't give anything a second thought."

They didn't sleep, and at 5:30 A.M., mist over the pond, they went skinny-dipping. The swans hardly bothered waking.

Honeymoon

WHEN THE Fasten Seatbelt signs blinkered out twenty minutes from Heathrow, William leaned across the aisle, said to Maggie, "Marrying your mother — rest in peace. Your birth. Your wedding. Those occasions notwithstanding. I've looked forward to meeting Mr. Aston more than anything else. I'm allowed just two hours of his time. But lord's sake, I've got a list of questions a mile long."

"I'm happy for you, Pop," Maggie said. "Things will turn out well."

"And I'm happy for you," he said. He looked at David, asleep in his window seat. "Happy for David, too, that he married so well."

In London, Maggie and David got situated in their room at Durrants Hotel; William went directly to his bed-and-breakfast near the Kensington Market. First thing, he left a message with Reginald Aston's secretary, confirming the appointment.

The next morning William slept late, then set forth being a tourist. His happiness at wandering the streets of London was tempered by his wife's absence. They'd not traveled much together. Still, over the next ten days he found it satisfying to jettison his habitual frugality and splurge, going to restaurants, the theater (seeing two plays by Harold Pinter, commenting during the one Islay-to-London call from Maggie, "His characters all talk pared down, like Newfoundlanders. Wonderful stuff") and museums. He spent an afternoon in Regent's Park. He visited Churchill's underground war headquarters. He didn't know a soul in London; his days and evenings were solitary; he enjoyed himself immensely.

The newlyweds had hired a car to take them to the early afternoon ferry from the Caledonian MacBrayne terminal at Kennacraig, on the Argyll mainland, which docked at Port Askaig on Islay. Isador Tecosky met them with his car and drove them to Port Charlotte, where they checked in to the Port Charlotte Hotel. Beautiful sea view out onto Loch Indaal. They spent the next afternoon with Stefania and Isador at their house, in the village of Eilean Dubh. It was of course the first time David had met them. That night, sitting on the rim of the bathtub in their hotel room as the bath filled, Maggie said to David, sitting cross-legged on the floor, "They've never been not kind. Never not, and I must've tested their patience, being a stubborn kid. I caught myself staring at them today, sort of a trance of remembering. I didn't even offer to help with coffee. I haven't seen them in quite a while. Especially Stefania, but both are slowed down so much, those creaky old bones. Stefania forgets things left and right. And I do not like Izzy's cough, either. But they are dear, dear people. The dearest to me. They gave my mom and dad a life in so many ways."

The next morning broke sunny and clear. Their waitress in the hotel's dining room said, "Weather might change momentarily, but we try to enjoy what's given." She put in their order.

"Quit your job, Maggie," David said. "I know you like it. I know it's a good job, you've worked hard at it, but quit it. I told the Tate I'm moving to Halifax. I gave notice. But let's not go to Halifax. You give notice to Dalhousie. Let's stay here."

"And do what?"

"Not leave."

"And after that?"

"Keep not leaving."

They moved on to David's book proposal (he hadn't men-

tioned it all summer), then to their plans for the day, unfold-
ing the map of Islay on the table, folding it back up when
their breakfast was served. Just as they'd left a tip, they
looked out the window and witnessed a kind of incident: a
vintage black sedan, an ornamental silver bugle fixed to its
hood, passed by on the road in front of the hotel. An elderly
woman, black hair cut to just below her ears, her somber attention aimed straight ahead, was behind the wheel. A live
swan was in the back seat, also facing forward. The waitress,
come to fetch her tip and clear the table, saw this too. "Oh,
that's Mrs. Robert Campbell," she said. "That swan's got
clipped wings. Mrs. Campbell found it injured near her
house and nursed it back to health. She's devoted to it beyond the logical, and why? Because she thinks the swan's her
dear departed husband. What's the harm, I say. And besides,
when Mrs. Campbell looks at that swan, who's to tell her
Mr. Campbell shouldn't come to mind? Who's to judge?"

David said, "We should all be so lucky," clearly surprised
at himself, as if he'd stated a belief in the afterlife he didn't
know he held. He looked at Maggie, who said, "Now that's a
topic of conversation, isn't it? For later, darling." The waitress went to another table.

Such an odd sight might have conveniently convinced a
tourist of the general notion of Scottish eccentricity, or in
this case, eccentricity on Islay in particular. But for all David
and Maggie knew, the waitress considered the sight of Mrs.

Campbell chauffeuring her swan-husband as merely familiar.

"Well, my part of Nova Scotia's got its share of people equally fixed in their beliefs, of this and that sort," Maggie said.

"You're not homesick, are you?" David said.

"Not in the least. Not here. Not now."

After breakfast they called on the Tecoskys again, inviting them out for a walk. They'd strolled along the cliffs for only ten minutes or so when Isador got winded and began coughing. They returned to the house. "Some days are easier than others," he said. "What can I tell you?"

"You live in a beautiful place," David said. "Your house is the most comfortable I've ever been in in my life. I mean that."

In their kitchen Isador presented them with a pair of binoculars. "May we suggest your going to look at swans," Stefania said. "They're called whooper swans, and they arrived early this year. You can see them at Loch Gorm. Please use our car. We aren't driving anywhere all week."

They visited the Round Church in Bowmore, built in 1767, one of two round churches in Scotland. The medieval ruined chapel and grave slabs at Finlaggan. The old Islay lifeboat station at Port Askaig. They drove all over the island. Lochs and harbor villages. But every day, too, they stopped at a different beach. The one at Lossit, at

Kilchiaran, Saligo, Tayvulin, Aros, Traigh Bhan, Big Strand; much of their time made for a kind of gazetteer of beaches; the sea set up its lull and roar in their ears. Their map of Islay was creased, frayed, marked up with directions, blotched with tea stains.

They reluctantly left Islay on August 18, this time flying from Glendale to Glasgow, then to London, arriving at Durrants Hotel at 1 A.M. Since Maggie's flight to Amsterdam (with connecting flights to Montreal and Halifax) was at 7 A.M., they decided to stay up all night, which they did. Then David drove Maggie to Heathrow.

David went back to the hotel. He slept till noon, waking because the telephone rang. It was William. He was in the lobby. David joined him for lunch in the dining room. William spoke excitedly about his appointment with Mr. Aston, asked after Stefania and Isador, of course asked after Maggie, and finally said he intended that afternoon to visit the Tower of London, then make an early night of it. David noticed that when William got worked up in his enthusiasms, his Scottish accent intensified. He also noted that William pointedly did not ask how "they" enjoyed their honeymoon — he'd phrased it, "And how'd Maggie like things on Islay?" *He's getting used to the idea of us being married*, David thought. *Nothing unusual there.* On the other hand, William thought, *Look at this, he lets me rattle on — po-*

liteness for the old father-in-law — he'll learn how to speak up for himself with me — then it'll be a real conversation — things take time. David picked up the tab without need of insistence. "Not much to spend your money on on Islay, is there?" William said.

"See you soon in Parrsboro," David said. They shook hands. "Then we'll hear all about your visit with the Queen's swankeeper."

They took separate cabs, William to the Tower of London, David to his bank, where he transferred all but a little of his savings to a bank in Halifax. He ran a few other errands. By the time he got back to Durrants Hotel, it was 5:45. The instant his cab stopped in front of the hotel, he saw Katrine Novak entering the lobby. He was incredulous: although he might better have thought, *Don't go into the hotel,* he actually thought, *We should never have left Islay.* Neither was quite useful enough. He paid the cabbie and went into the lobby, where Katrine was inquiring after him at the registration desk.

"Katrine," David said. She turned and they stared at each other across the lobby. "What are you doing here?" David's sour tone drew John Franco's disapproving notice. David locked his arm in Katrine's and steered her to the bar. They sat at a corner table.

Katrine was thirty-one, slim, as tall as David, with dark

brown hair cut short, a beautiful complexion, cheekbones with wide-angled planes, brown eyes. An altogether striking woman. She was dressed in what David called, with dubious affection, one of her "Eastern European bohemian looks": black jeans, buckled ankle-length boots, black cowboy shirt with silver piping. She spoke English with a noticeable but not thick accent. She was a freelance translator, mainly of mystery novels, "killer-thrillers," as she called them, police procedurals like Ed McBain's. Translation fees varied, and steady work didn't necessarily mean the bills got paid on time. An acquaintance at the Tate once asked David to describe the woman he was seeing in Prague, and he said, "Beautiful and matter-of-fact." But Katrine was more complicated than that. Like anyone is more complicated.

"I got your letter," she said. "I take it David Kozol is married. Did your life work out this way?"

"Katrine, first, how did you find me?"

"Well —" She took a pack of cigarettes from her pocketbook, tapped one out, flicked her lighter and smoked for a moment. "You see, that question puts me in the position of humiliation. Because if I answer it honestly, I have to describe how I spent much precious time to find you, which is true. You didn't have your telephone machine hooked up for months, right? Finally I called the gallery where you teach. Your friend there — someone, what's his name, I forgot —

said you were flying here to Canada, back and forth. Doing this a lot, he said. He said why not knock on your apartment door. I waited these months. I had my work. I accepted you wanted to end things. But then I asked myself, How do I feel dignified in this? Okay, so we were never to get married maybe. Fine and dandy, all right. However, you got to write your letter, but I don't get to answer? I decided it's best in person. So I called your gallery friend back. He gave me your landlord's telephone, who I rang. And he said you just stopped in to pay some money you owed him. He said you were checked into this Durrants Hotel. Simple. I went to the airport and now I'm here."

"I am married, Katrine. I married Margaret."

"I'm happy for you. I'm not happy for you."

"I understand."

"Really? In your letter you wrote you *hope* to be married, but no letter after said you were married. That would have been useful, David."

Katrine opened her small travel bag, took out a stack of photographs held together by a rubber band. She threw them at David, hitting him in the chest. They scattered on the floor. David leaned over and picked them up. "All these you took of me. I looked at them over the past months, my copies you gave me. They are every possible fucking cliché of Prague, every kind of not-original shit, David. Katrine at

Kafka's grave. Katrine at the Jewish cemetery. Katrine in this garden, Katrine in that beer hall. My God, what I let you turn me into. The city I was born in!"

"You came all this way to tell me I'm a second-rate photographer?"

"That would only be kind. No, I'm saying — and it's just like you not to see it. I am saying you took photographs which associated me with *predictable* surroundings. Is this over your head? Maybe it is. So, it occurred to me you all along felt I was part of *predictable* life. Still, I liked spending time with you, David, even some of the nights. Some of them, my friend."

"I —"

"Let me ask you something. Did you tell your Margaret about me? Did you tell this new wife about me? If you didn't, perhaps somewhere deep down you haven't really left me yet. Though don't flatter yourself, it wouldn't matter."

"No, I didn't feel any need to tell her."

"Need. Want. Hope. All such bullshit. You know what I always thought? All those talks we had, when you spoke all that — how to say it? *Self-deprecation.* See, I'm not a translator for nothing, huh? I found the right word. All that self-deprecation you like so much, David. I've concluded it's all actually a form of self-regard, 'the wonder of me' bullshit."

"We had a lot of good conversations, Katrine. Come on, they weren't all —"

"I think what I think."

Katrine smoked and David stared off at the wall, out the window. "You know," she said, "just now, I feel in my stomach it was bad fortune to see you again. Maybe a mistake. Except it was important to me — and my boyfriend Pavel agreed, by the way. Important to me to not send you a letter, but to look at your face. Not be the coward with a letter."

"There's probably a flight to Prague tonight."

"No, I'm going to look at London a day or two. I thought it might take that long to find you. I have a room elsewhere."

"I'm sorry you came all this way, Katrine. I meant well with my letter."

"How can such a letter mean well? An idiot would say such a thing." She reached into her purse again, took out David's letter, along with other sheets of paper with Czech writing on them. "By the way, I'm publishing my translation of your letter to me."

"What are you talking about?"

"Look." She held up the Czech pages. "Yes, I got back to writing stories, like I used to before I started translating. A few editors asked if I had anything. This inspired me to try again. So, I took much of the summer to work on a story. A very good journal has accepted it. I was paid for it. Pavel likes it very much. It's about a man and woman who fall in love, then fall hard out of it; his name is David Kozol. Hers is not Katrine. Anyway, she finally — how do you say it? *Dumps* this David. But he cannot take it, so he writes a letter — this is your letter to me, word for word. I translated it out on my typewriter. He shows all his friends this letter, to try and prove he is a very reasonable, nice man. They all never wish to see him again. That's my ending. It should be published soon. December, I think."

"You can't be telling me the truth, Katrine."

"Maybe yes, maybe no — what difference? You can't read it anyway. Unless you pay me to translate it."

They sat through Katrine's smoking another cigarette. David ordered a glass of whiskey, then a second. Katrine drank a vodka. They didn't speak much at all. At last Katrine said, "I think you can't be too sad to see me, David. Because why? Because you haven't got up to go to your room, have you?"

"Neither sad nor happy, Katrine. Just taken aback."

"Know what *I* am? I am tired and hungry. How about it, David, dinner with an old friend? I will telephone my Pavel and tell him I'm having dinner with you. He'll appreciate that I told him."

"I don't think dinner's a good idea."

"I *hate* good ideas. You know this about me."

David smiled at her familiar contrariness.

"I'm hungry, too, I suppose. Dinner, then you'll get a cab to your hotel, right?"

She went to the telephone booth in the hallway and called Pavel. He was a doctor. She reached him at his office. After describing how she'd "looked David Kozol in the eye," she said, "It's nothing, really. It's only dinner." Pavel told her that he had a patient waiting; that he loved her; that he would pick her up at the airport, just let him know when.

They took a table near the window. "The truth is, David, you were so seldom in Prague," she said. "And I never came to London. I never suggested I visit you in London. You never asked. This not asking went on for four years, almost." The waiter came to the table. Katrine said, "Your best Italian Chianti, please." The waiter nodded approval and went into the kitchen. When the wine was poured, Katrine clinked her glass against David's, said, "To old times. Means, we tried each other out and lived to tell the tale, yes?" But they didn't tell any tales, not really. They ate in pretty much a comfortable silence. They shared a second bottle. No dessert. "Coffee in your room, my friend, David," Katrine said. "Then I'll get my taxicab."

"Katrine, how about coffee in the bar?"

"Be *polite*, David. I traveled a long ways to say goodbye in person. I'll say it over coffee, then get my cab."

In his room, Katrine sat on the sofa, David in the chair opposite her. A bottle of wine, compliments of the hotel, sat on the glass-topped table in between. Katrine opened it, poured them each a glass. Room service delivered a pot of coffee. They didn't pour any yet. On they talked. What about, David, only a day later, couldn't remember. Mostly, increasingly drunken non sequiturs. They dozed off, startled awake, the room a kind of emotional purgatory; neither was particularly animated; no buttons got unbuttoned; they eventually fell asleep. David in the chair, Katrine on the sofa. Yet here was the thing, of course: the fact of Katrine's being in David's hotel room — the fact from which every consequent form of collapse emanated — meant David had dropped Maggie's trust, whether she ever found out about it or not. True, the evening constituted David and Katrine's final parting of ways, but it had taken place *after* his marriage to Maggie. This chronology offered its own judgment.

The hotel room, with its metallic-tasting water, a pocket of rust somewhere along the pipes, nicely appointed as it was.

William knocked on David's door at 7:55 in the morning. This was August 19, the day William had his noon appointment with Reginald Aston, royal swankeeper. Katrine heard the knock just as she stepped from the shower. She'd felt grubby and hung over — disgusting, really — but was in fairly good humor. She'd put on the plush terrycloth robe provided by the hotel and opened the door. William was dressed in a brown corduroy sports jacket with elbow patches, a white shirt, khaki trousers, sensible walking shoes. He was holding a small gift-wrapped package. Katrine held open the door and said, "Yes?"

William looked at Katrine's face, admired it. He noticed especially her skin, a bit flushed from the steam; the bathrobe was more than evident. Then he looked past her and saw David groaning awake. Katrine said, "David, this man is definitely perhaps not a stranger to you, I think. Should he come in, then?"

David stood up in his rumpled clothes and looked at William. "David," William said, not moving from the doorway but holding up the box. "I thought you might bring this to Margaret. It's a small vase with real dragonflies somehow blown into it. I was told the fact it was made in 1890 warranted the price."

"She'll like it very much," David said.

"I've suddenly changed my mind. Now I think it's best I give this vase to my daughter in person. When I get back to Canada." His voice held a kind of stark conviction, but his face betrayed little. He grasped the doorknob, didn't offer Katrine the least further acknowledgment, backed out into the hallway and solidly shut the door behind him.

Tightening its belt and holding the robe closed at the neck, Katrine looked at a stunned David, then said, "Oh, I see in your face you certainly yes are married."

Wrenched by William's presence, still brain-muddled from

all the wine, and with what Katrine felt to be an almost comic franticness, David flew into action. He looked for his shoes, found them in the bathroom, not recalling how they'd got there. He splashed cold water on his face, then took some deep breaths. He pressed his forehead to the mirror above the sink, as if to keep thoughts inside, and said to himself, "We saw a swan in a car together, in the Hebrides." He pounded the mirror with his fist. It might have shattered, but didn't.

As Katrine got dressed, what sprung to her mind — she being constantly susceptible to literary references — was the English title of a novel by Louisa May Alcott she'd translated into Czech, *A Long Fatal Love Chase*. She said the title aloud with world-weary resignation, as if it somehow forecasted what David had now begun as he hurried past her into the hallway. He raced down the stairs and out onto George Street, observed by John Franco and the concierge. He ran toward the intersection where he knew William could catch a bus, or, fueled by whatever William might be fueled by — rage, disappointment, disgust, sadness, the combinations were interminable — could easily begin a crosstown walk. David had chosen correctly: he caught immediate sight of William, of all things just sitting at a café table, like any man out for breakfast. A cup of tea and a muffin were on the table, along with the gift-wrapped box.

"William," David said, approaching the table.

William looked up, took David in, stood, and without a moment's hesitation lifted the cup and flung its contents. Tea splashed against David's chest. He winced in pain but continued forward, grasped William's shoulders and said, "Please, listen. William, there was nothing —" True and not true. William grabbed hold of David's shirt and pushed him backward, letting go. David careened against a nearby table but didn't fall.

"What are my choices?" William said. He stepped forward and took a wild swing, which David easily ducked. One of the two women standing behind the pastry counter shouted, "Stop it, you bloody idiots!" The other had already picked up the wall telephone and dialed the police. "Go on, both of you — get out of here!"

William and David seemed almost calmly to escort each other out of the café, but once on the street, William took another swing, which David deflected downward, grabbing and yanking William's arm so that his father-in-law fell to the sidewalk. William quickly got to his feet. David held his hands palms-out and said, "William, just listen, will you, please?"

David moved forward. William moved back and stumbled off the curb, severely twisting his left ankle. He crumpled into the street. A cabbie (his name was Derek Moreland, age fifty-six), moments before, had picked up Katrine Novak in front of Durrants Hotel. He'd just glanced at her in the rearview mirror when she shouted, "Watch it!" She had recognized William ahead in the street but hadn't noticed David. The cabbie turned to the front and said, "Fuck-all!" He leaned on the horn and braked hard but the cab thudded into William, who was trying to lift himself up.

Katrine was thrown against the front seat. The cabbie said, "You all right?" She speechlessly nodded yes, but was obviously shaken. "The fellow possibly ain't dead, miss." But he could not know either way. He issued instructions to Katrine: "You stay and give a statement. Not my fault, see. The gentleman stepped right out in front of me." Which was not exactly the case, as William was already in the street, though only for a split second. And it was an intersection. The cabbie turned off the ignition, pocketed the keys, got out of his taxi and walked to where William lay in the street. David shoved him. The cabbie said, "Hey, what? I was just —" and backed up a few steps. Katrine needed some air; she got out and leaned against the cab. "Ciggie," she advised herself, reaching into her handbag for a cigarette. She smoked, staring at the people gathered on the sidewalk.

David had in fact thought William was dead; there was blood at his mouth, his eyes stared up vacantly. Yet when David got on his knees and leaned close, William suddenly focused and grotesquely croaked, "Tell Mr. Aston I'll be late."

The ambulance arrived in less than ten minutes. Three

paramedics spilled out, attended to William. One asked William a question, said to the others, "He can't get out the words, mates." The youngest paramedic reported this and more to a doctor on standby over a kind of walkie-talkie, listened, then said, "Got it, got it, got it. Right." He placed the walkie-talkie in its holster on his belt. The paramedics conferred a moment, then fit a plastic collar around William's neck.

"Here we go, then," one said, and all scrupulously lifted William sideways onto a stretcher, carried the stretcher to the ambulance. One paramedic got in behind the wheel, a second sat in front on the passenger's side, the last climbed in back. David said, "I'm his son-in-law." The paramedic in back said, "Right, then," so David boosted himself up and sat next to William. Siren. Faces blurred past. On the sprint to the hospital the paramedic said, "Don't try to talk, sir," and hooked up an IV just as William blacked out.

Skywritten

THE FIRST WEEK of October 1986, a letter accepting David's book proposal, *Light and Dark: The Photographs of Josef Sudek*, arrived from Harrison Macomb. In fact, it was the second letter Macomb had sent. The first, back in June 1985, was forwarded to the Tate Gallery by David's landlord. The Tate had no recourse but to send it back to Macomb. David had pretty much cut off all of his old contacts. "I thought perhaps you'd become a bellman at Durrants Hotel and given up writing altogether!" Macomb wrote. "You seemed so at home in their lobby. But I'm told I've now found the proper address. At any rate, Mr. Kozol, I trust you still wish to write your book. You must ring me up and we'll discuss terms. Please know that I can offer a decent advance, but cannot make you a fortune unless the book makes me one. That said, your proposal was quite brilliant. I read closely and admired your other writings on Sudek. My staff thought highly of them as well."

David telephoned Macomb the next morning at 5 A.M., Nova Scotia time. Full of apologies, he said he'd gotten married and was now living in Canada, and added the lie that in between he'd been doing research. "My wife's expecting our first child in November," David said. "But I can certainly begin organizing my notes and get to work on the writing in, say, December."

"I don't tell my authors how to schedule their time, Mr. Kozol, but let's try to settle on a reasonable deadline, shall we? I prefer not editing until a first draft is completed. I've worked different ways with different writers, but that's my preference. Might that suit you?"

"This is my first book, but it sounds fine."

"Tecosky Estate, Parrsboro, Nova Scotia — still your address?"

"Yes."

"Good. Well, busy day here, Mr. Kozol, busy day in progress. Congratulations, finally. Glad to have caught up with you. A contract will be sent within a month. Look it over."

"Thank you very much, Mr. Macomb."

"Lunch again at Durrants when you're next in town?"

"Of course."

That afternoon near the pond, David showed Macomb's letter to William. "I take it you'd like me to report this to Margaret?" he said. "But good for you. Some form of employment, at least, when you most need it, whatever your and my daughter's living arrangements. Maybe write to Isador and Stefania. Thank them for letting me keep you on. I think once the child's born, a modest raise in salary might be forthcoming. Considering their devotion to Margaret."

All over Nova Scotia, the heat wave continued without reprieve through October. Some days were tolerable, others stifling, the nights on average fifteen to twenty degrees warmer than what was typical of the season. On the health front, William now walked up and down the stairs for exercise; he'd extended his daily constitutional, half a mile from the mailbox along Route 2 and back. His voice therapy had ended; he was reading articles from *National Geographic*, and sea and island tales by Robert Louis Stevenson and Joseph Conrad, aloud in a moderate voice at night in bed. "Nothing like being read to," he'd joked to Maggie. His primary anodyne was aspirin (also a glass of whiskey before sleep).

As for David, his bruises — brought about by what William referred to as the "Edinburgh–Parrsboro Express," as if he'd been waiting since childhood to throw a punch with such resolve behind it — lingered in lighter hues, and his jaw was still a bit numb. William had a folder of suggested recipes, provided by the hospital, and during the first few weeks of his son-in-law's recovery, he had used an electric blender to prepare concoctions of meat, vegetables and vitamins in liquid form, which David ate mostly through a straw. On October 21 David had his jaw unwired, an arduous procedure that required an anesthetic. William took him home from the hospital at 3 P.M. in the truck, a sudden deep rut in the road jolting David's skull like a relapse. Once in the guesthouse, David immediately took to his bed, and slept until four the next morning. He woke hearing static from the radio.

A few days later, William sat with David at the guesthouse's kitchen table, eating a dinner of egg salad sandwiches, soft pear slices and ice water. They said little during the meal. David cleared the dishes and they repaired to the porch, where David pressed an ice pack to the side of his face. They sat in opposite porch swings, feet planted on the slat floor. "Both these swings need oiling," William said.

"I'll get to it," David said.

They sat not talking for a good fifteen minutes, looking out toward the pond. Then William said, "Children's zoo keeps asking for our swans, but I told them as long as this heat keeps up, I prefer they stay here with us."

William had got the swans in the pen before dinner; he'd seen a fox crossing to the estate side of Route 2. At about seven o'clock there was the slightest of breezes. Veering in from the north, all at once there arrived a flock of wild swans. In successive groups of six, eight and ten, they settled in the pond with scarcely a splash, spreading out with impressive equanimity over its breadth. From his vantage point William saw their initial approach; David turned in time to see them light. "Those are whistling swans. *Cygnus columbianus.* Naomi said they got here late August last year," William said. "Let's go down and have a look."

They walked past the pen. The Tecoskys' swans were worked up, a number of them with bills pressed to the fence. Their abbreviated wings and confinement seemed cruel. The whistlings continued to converge. The wild swans were on high alert; they formed a loose-knit gather, the biggest ones in a kind of half circle, facing outward.

"Let's move back a little," William said, "even though they're unlikely to scare off." Still, they had a fine view, and each in his own fashion felt it was an exhilarating sight. "Looking at them, you can get fooled into thinking the whole world's working right." Behind them the Tecoskys' swans were moving loudly about their pen, yet the whistlings now all appeared to be sleeping. "I can't imagine how bone-tired they must get. I saw swans out of an airplane once."

"Where was that?" David asked.

"Right here over Nova Scotia. I went up in a small airplane with John Pallismore. He was a skywriting expert. Now that's a story."

"I imagine I'm going to hear it."

"Keep looking at these wild swans. It'll get you through."

"Go ahead, William. Really, I'm all ears."

"This was in 1972. I remember, because we'd hired someone, just for a few weeks, to clear brush and paint both porches. This fellow Sam shows up. No automobile. No money to speak of. Samuel Oliver — dodging the American draft, didn't want the Vietnam conflict to murder him or otherwise postpone his life, was morally opposed, which he and I agreed on one hundred percent. Not everyone in Parrsboro did.

"Anyway, back to seeing swans from a plane. The thing is, you needed a special license to skywrite with an airplane. There was just John and one other fellow with skywriting licenses in the entire province. John was also our local mail carrier, all up and down Route 2. He supplemented his income with skywriting, though not much. The mainstay of his skywriting work came out of Halifax, where the money was. He'd be hired to help launch some business or other. The time in question, I flew from Truro to Halifax with him. His job that day was to spell out the name of a new hotel above Halifax Harbor. The plane was specially fitted for this purpose, and I joked it was like flying a big cigar, smoking all on its own, a cigar that could spell and write. Anyway, flying back to the airstrip near Truro was when we saw the wild swans high up, pretty close by."

"That's the story?"

"No, that's just when I saw the swans. The *story* is, John Pallismore had a high school sweetheart named Ellen Tanning. And John had been smitten without decline after high school as well. It was unrequited, though. Ellen simply could not return John's affection, eh? And as if that wasn't problem enough for him, when Ellen married locally, she and her husband — Eammon — set up house in Upper Economy right along John's mail route.

"That meant John had to stop by Ellen's house every day but Sunday. This was torture for John. He delivered mail to the life he wanted, but he himself wasn't living it.

"Ellen and Eammon had a daughter, Elsa-Louise, plus they'd adopted Ellen's niece at age five, Mildred, who'd been orphaned. She came to live with them and fit right in. They weathered things well. The four of them attended church together and such.

"Then, when it was approaching Ellen's thirty-fifth birthday, Eammon hired John Pallismore to skywrite a birthday message out over the Bay of Fundy. They worked out terms. John always got half up front, half when the job was done, if every word was readable. On Ellen's birthday there was a social going on in Parrsboro, lots of people on the church lawn, which was how Eammon planned it — you want people to see your matrimonial devotion at work. And when all those people looked up, there's the words HAPPY BIRTHDAY ELLEN, loud and clear and so beautifully written, like the heavens themselves were communicating.

"Except. *Except* — it was signed, LOVE, comma, JOHN. Not LOVE, EAMMON, but LOVE, JOHN.

"No big secret, really. I mean everybody in Parrsboro already knew John was madly in love with Ellen and always had been. But his declaration of it was kind of new. Well, first thing, the church social breaks up — people went right home. Secondly, the next day Eammon petitioned through official lines to get John's skywriting license revoked. Next, thirdly, and this everyone agreed was a good decision, John Pallismore had to switch mail routes with a man named Sander Malachy. That was smart of the postal system, wasn't it, to avoid all sorts of problems. You don't want a murder — not that Eammon was capable of such a thing. He must've felt murderous, though. Family embarrassment displayed on the world's biggest billboard like that.

"The minister of the church offered that John might consider skywriting an apology of sorts. Well, John picked right up on that advice. He got the skywriting apparatus ship-shape and up he went, same part of the sky, whereupon he wrote: ELLEN I HAVE LOVED YOU FOREVER, comma, JOHN.

"Oh, my goodness, a skywritten sentence can stay intact floating out there quite a long time, let me tell you, depending on wind conditions. And this time John had done it on his own nickel, so he could write whatever he pleased. Of course, he'd written what he'd pleased the first time too, hadn't he?

"Next, Eammon drove the family down to visit cousins in Port Medway for a week. Took the girls right out of school. And when they got back to Upper Economy, John drove up to their mailbox and delivered — and this is the amount rumored — two thousand love letters he'd written to Ellen since high school but had never sent. Stacked them neatly bundled.

"At this point, and without special encouragement, John committed himself to Nova Scotia Hospital, there in Dartmouth, for observation. Much to his credit. He just sized his mind up, drove to Halifax, parked his car, took the ferry over and got a room there, he said, like he'd checked into a hotel. Thirty days worked. Now he's living in Yarmouth. Needless to say, he's no longer delivering mail. He's employed, last I heard, at the ferry terminal in some capacity."

"He landed on his feet, then, John Pallismore," David said.

"Basically," William said.

They watched the wild swans for a few more minutes and then William said, "Just out of curiosity, David. Which person in that true story do you consider most wronged by life?"

"The children, I suppose," David said. "Is there a reason you told me that story, William?"

"Margaret always loved it. She thought somebody should write an opera. The first opera set in Nova Scotia."

They stayed with the wild swans till dark, then returned to opposite porch swings. Sitting down, William said, "I can't stand it another minute." He went inside, brought out a can of 3-in-One oil, thoroughly oiled then tested both swings, returned the oil to the house and joined David back on the porch.

"I said I was going to get to it," David said.

"Now you don't have to."

They didn't want to leave the wild swans. Managing only small talk, they mainly looked toward the pond until late into dusk. Then William said, "I've got a directive from Margaret and she hopes you'll follow it."

"Directive?"

"My word, not my daughter's."

"What is this directive, then?"

"You can look at her through the window," William said.

"But she doesn't want you to come out and speak to her or anything. You just keep to the house."

"Pretty much the status quo, isn't it?"

"Status quo, except for the baby rounding out, as the saying goes. What's changed is that you don't have to leave the estate and drive around through two tanks of gas till Margaret leaves anymore. Actually, the directive's her way of asking you *not* to leave, is my interpretation."

"And should she happen to saunter past the guesthouse? To go swimming, say?"

"It's the common-most way to get there, isn't it? She and I might walk by. Or she alone. Maybe to swim. With this ungodly heat, and what with pregnancy being uncomfortable enough as it is. I remember Janice practically lived in that pond the summer Maggie was born."

"I don't get it. Maggie's not cruel. I don't recognize her in this so-called directive."

"Start recognizing her in it, is my advice, take it or leave it. Consider it a way she keeps control, buys herself a little time to figure things out. A camera works through a window — take the opportunity to start your family album."

"Will she take me back, William? I am asking directly. Once the baby's born?"

"In my opinion, based on nothing but my opinion, she's considering it. If I were you — God help me — if I were you, I'd comply. Don't comply, well, I'm fit as a fiddle now, almost. I can drive the truck again. I can visit my daughter in Halifax. She doesn't have to travel up here. But consider things on her behalf: the estate's peaceful for her, with the possible exception of your presence."

"I see."

"The word 'directive' now fits like a glove, doesn't it?"

"When's Maggie visiting next?"

"Not until two days from now. Saturday. It's a work week. She still works for a living."

"If I write out a list, will you pick up some film for me? I'm not supposed to drive on these painkillers."

"I'll do it first thing tomorrow."

"Thank you."

"Margaret is quite capable of raising a daughter on her own. Don't think for a minute she isn't. And don't think for a minute she won't. Patience, I'm sure, will be useful in this situation, David, but don't count on patience alone to provide results you think are fair, or any other such goddamn nonsense like fairness. Jesus, man, what's *wrong* with you? You've got everything to lose. You've got to act on your feelings for Margaret best you can. *Do* something besides *thinking*." William got up from his porch swing; it squeaked a little and both men laughed. "Anyway, just put the list on the front seat of the truck. You'll fend for breakfast yourself,

eh? I guess orange juice and toast won't challenge you beyond your present abilities."

The wild swans left on Saturday morning at dawn. During
their occupation of the pond, the Tecoskys' swans were con-
fined to the pen. David had sprayed them with a hose four
times a day. Maggie arrived to the estate at 10:15 A.M. David
had stayed up the entire night before, nervous about seeing
his own wife. Since 7:30 A.M., after freeing the swans from
the pen, he had stood at the window. He ate breakfast standing there. Drank coffee. Cleaned his telephoto lens. Now,
looking through the kitchen window as she slowly emerged
from her car, David saw that Maggie was wearing a loose-
knit pair of slacks, a white blouse and black flats. She stopped
halfway to the porch, turned toward the guesthouse, placed
her hands, fingers splayed, on her considerable belly and
gazed at them. Then she went into the main house.

David took up his Nikon from the table. The kitchen
window looked out on a wider stretch of lawn than any
other in the guesthouse, and therefore allowed the longest
duration of time he might view Maggie, should she walk
to the pond and back. At 11:50 William and Maggie did
walk to the pond. William carried a picnic basket. David at-
tached the telephoto lens. Maggie wore a skirted one-piece
swimsuit obviously designed for pregnant women, and David thought she looked wonderful. He noticed that she ap-

peared a touch weary around the eyes. Their pace was leisurely and they didn't hesitate in the least while passing the guesthouse. Nor did Maggie look over. David snapped six photographs, the final one capturing Maggie and William entirely from the back.

When they reached the pond, Maggie pointed at the swans; two were on the water, the rest on the far bank, sleeping, preening, the usual repertoire. William removed the loafer from his left foot, dipped his toes in, testing the water. He said something to Maggie. She carefully waded in. David could hear her laughter through the screen door. Submerged up to her waist, she stretched out across the surface and performed a few sidestrokes, drifted, stroked out to the middle and back. David took photographs all along from the porch. Maggie got out of the water. David photographed their picnic, a few swans paddling close for handouts, receiving none.

William walked back to the main house. David went into his kitchen. Replacing the telephoto lens with a shorter one, David photographed Maggie as she walked past half an hour later. She combed her fingers through her hair, twisted the ends, ringing out pond water. When she was directly in front of the kitchen window, she stopped. Maggie allowed David to chronicle her braiding her hair into two pigtails, and then, without once meeting his eyes, she continued on.

This tableau — David behind a window, Maggie just outside — constituted part of the same choreography of punishment and encouragement that defined each of Maggie's visits over the next few weeks, and raised in William's mind questions about what inventive stupidities people were capable of when wounded and confused, no matter their native intelligence. No matter their love for each other.

He'd come to some new knowledge about his daughter, always a useful thing, he knew. He thought about her situation most often at night while listening to opera. On the one hand, he admired her having built such a forbidding moat around herself. Why should she let David easily cross it? They had not even had time to set up house, and then that London hotel room. Dunce. On the other hand, William worried that her visits — this directive, et cetera — had a recklessness about them. That Maggie's appearances and exhibitions, these opportunities for David to begin their family album under house arrest, contained a taunting vindictiveness he previously had no idea was part of his daughter's nature, and whether justified or not, such displays might erode the situation beyond repair. Though nothing could be concluded with certainty, he figured that obsessing like this partly defined being a father, in that he was obliged to think these thoughts but could not — except when asked, and even then he'd expect his opinions to be ignored — give advice to Maggie. Besides, what could he do about any of this? He tried not to lose sleep over it. But a person doesn't get to choose what to lose sleep over.

When Maggie disappeared into the house, David went straight to the darkroom, spending hours developing the photographs. To his great relief they all were in focus. He hung the prints on a clothesline in the bathroom to dry, and later fitted each one in the album William had purchased in Parrsboro. Under each photograph, along with the date, he provided a simple caption: "Maggie opening a picnic basket," "Maggie looking at swans," "Maggie asleep on a blanket," and so on. The captions served no purpose other than to describe the obvious. As for the photographs themselves, they qualified more as snapshots than anything. In this respect, they defied all influence of Josef Sudek, but were hardly original. Too bad: clichés often have some ring of truth; these were scenes he embraced. David's photographs were constructions of memory, the album meant to preserve them, and he considered it a decent beginning.

Late Sunday morning, after taking photographs of Maggie walking to her car as she left for Halifax, David didn't submit to any pain medication and drove the truck into Parrsboro for an early lunch at Minas Bakery. He'd telephoned William first, asking to use the truck, and William's reply was "It's low on gas, you'll notice."

The bakery was empty of customers. Dory Elliot was washing the pastry window, which she once referred to as "the best view in Parrsboro." The window was full of lemon tarts, baked that morning. She got to the bakery at 4 A.M., as everyone knew.

"How's life so far this morning?" she said to David when he sat down at a table.

"Coffee, please, Dory. And a tuna sandwich — and I know it's a bit early for lunch, but I was up early."

"You look like you were up all night."

"And a glass of water, please." Dory put a cup of coffee and a glass of water on the table, then set about preparing the sandwich. "Dory, I don't think I'm up to answering your 'How's life?' question. Sorry."

"Well, your face no longer resembles a Halloween mask. That's optimistic."

David noticed a paperback face-down on the counter. "What are you reading there?"

"Mr. Earl Stanley Gardner. A Perry Mason mystery. *The Case of the Dubious Bridegroom*. He wrote hundreds, and I've read dozens to date."

"I remember the American TV program."

"Nothing like the books," Dory said. "The TV show, I watched it religiously. But it was always the same. They got to the trial as soon as possible, and then, five minutes before the end, some man or woman — and sometimes you hadn't even seen this person before! — they'd stand up in the courtroom and cry out, 'I did it!' And Perry would turn those big dark owl eyes on that person and get an expression on his face, and there was only one possible way to interpret his expression: 'I knew it was you all along!' But like I said, I watched it religiously. And what do I mean by that? I mean had *Perry Mason* been broadcast on Sunday mornings, I would have chosen it over church."

"Since I've known you," David said, "you've always chosen not going to church, without any TV show conflicting."

"That's true too. But also I have my bakery open Sunday mornings. In case you hadn't noticed. I provide for people after church. I've been told more than once it's appreciated."

Dory lived over the bakery. She once said to David, "I'm the only one in Parrsboro travels vertically to work." He watched her make the sandwich, then looked out the window. The old-fashioned crank-down green-and-white-striped awning cast a shadow on the sidewalk. Dory brought over the sandwich, went back behind the counter. After taking a few bites, David noticed Dory staring at him. "What is it, Dory?" he said.

"Would you please tell me how William's doing?"

"Sit down with me a minute."

Dory stepped around the counter and sat across from David. "Thanks for the invitation," she said.

"William is much improved," David said. "Last doctor's

report was excellent. He's singing along with his opera records."

"Dead opera singers turning in their graves, I imagine."

"My father-in-law doesn't have much of a voice. But considering that after the accident he wasn't much more than a bullfrog with laryngitis —"

"What a thing, that accident. What a thing."

"I won't ask you, Dory, what you know of all that. Let's just say I'm aware Naomi Bloor stops into the bakery on a regular basis."

"Did you conjoin with that Czechoslovaki woman or not?"

"God, you are a direct person, aren't you?"

"Yes or no?"

"Yes, before Maggie and I were married. No, after."

Dory reached over and took a sip of David's coffee. "Before is before. After would've been entirely different, eh?"

"Dory —"

"Sandwich bad?"

"No, it's fine. Dory — William told me. About you and him."

"When?"

"When I was in the hospital. We were looking at Field family photograph albums. There were photographs of you in them. One subject led to another. I was getting morphine."

"I'd've asked for morphine myself, hearing that news. So

now you understand why I wasn't invited to the wedding. At least I got to bake the cake. That meant the world to me."

"Anyway —"

"I bet William didn't tell you, when Maggie called him out and she and Janice left for Halifax, William shot six swans with his father's shotgun from Scotland."

"That can't be true, Dory, the way he regards those swans."

"True as we're sitting here. I'd seen Maggie and Janice drive past about five-thirty that awful day. I locked up the bakery and drove right over to try and iron things out with William. Just when I arrived to the estate, I heard the blasts, got out of my car and set out for the pond. William walked right past me like I was a ghost. I went down to the pond and saw the swans floating dead. One, two, three, four, five, six. Counting them was the most convenient response, I guess, before the deeper truth of it set in."

Dory closed her eyes and shook her head, as if trying to clear it, then opened her eyes, brimmed with tears.

"You want me to sit with you awhile?" David said.

"No. No, I've got my paperback. Coffee and sandwich are on me, please. Water's always gratis."

David left the bakery.

Maggie made another visit on October 25. Midafternoon, David looked through the kitchen window and saw William drive off in the truck. Maggie appeared on the lawn shortly after. David had drunk several cups of coffee after eating a cheese sandwich, and his head was buzzing a little. He quickly got his lens adjusted and was about to photograph Maggie as she carried a towel to the pond, but he stopped and said to himself, "How many photographs of the same thing do I need?" Maggie swam at one end of the pond, with the unperturbed swans at the other. When she emerged, toweled off and walked up the slope, David was entirely unprepared for what happened next. Maggie stopped about twenty-five feet from the kitchen window. Bending with stilted gracefulness, she slipped out of her bathing suit and stood naked, looking directly at David. She placed her hands on her belly. Her breasts were fuller now; her face was fuller; her very spirit seemed fuller to David. His wife was an enthralling vision; he felt bereft of touch. He set the camera down and stared. *He's without a clue — still taking my directive*, she thought, *when he should come out of the house and hold me*. Maggie stood for a moment longer and then, towel wrapped around her, holding the suit, walked to the main house.

On October 27, late in the morning, David drove to Truro General Hospital for a final set of x-rays, which revealed that his jaw had completely healed. When he got back to the estate, he saw the postal service van just leaving. He parked the truck in front of the main house. "Hey, David," William called from the porch. "I want to show you something." David walked over. "The mail brought you good news the other day. Now it's brought me good news. How about that?"

"You referring to the letter you've got in your hand?"

"It's from Mr. Reginald Aston."

"Ah, the Queen's swankeeper."

"The fellow you broke my appointment with, correct. We've been back in correspondence for two months, give or take. But David, I need to ask you something. When I was half dead in the streets of London, what did I say? I remember saying something."

"'Tell Mr. Aston I'll be late.'"

"I said that?"

"Word for word."

"When I first wrote him, I made my excuses. His reply proved he isn't a man above accepting an apology. He asked after my health. And now he's confirmed a new appointment."

"You'll tell Maggie, I guess."

"Right away."

"She'll be very happy for you."

"Of course, I'll wait till the child's born before flying to London."

William began to read the letter again. As David walked off, William said, "I've set a tape recorder on your kitchen table. Margaret asked me to. You'll probably want to hear what's on it."

David hurried to the guesthouse, pressed the Play button on the tape recorder, sat at the table and listened to Maggie's voice:

David: First off, apparently I didn't mean enough to you that you would ever drive to my apartment here in Halifax and simply pound on my door until I answered or even wait out front of my building. Nor could you burden yourself to follow me to London or Amsterdam or anywhere else, once you'd found out which city the ensemble traveled to, which I know you did now and then because my faithful assistant Carol Emery told me. What sort of husband sorry for his actions would not do those things? What sort of husband? These are questions I've been asking myself. Have you asked them of yourself? Playing nursemaid to my father all these months — well, I'm sure it's kept you busy. And I know he's appreciated it, in his own way. In fact, I was glad you were there. But he's been able to take care of himself for some time now, hasn't he, and still you haven't once been to Halifax exclusively to see me. You drove down to see a movie and a play with Naomi Bloor but not to see your own wife. Anyway, since you did whatever you did or didn't do with whomever she was in your hotel room in London the very same day I departed our honeymoon for Halifax, I've gotten along. But I keep asking, lord in heaven, who is David Kozol to me now? My husband still on paper. Months back I actually listed the reasons I fell in love with you. One, I'd imagined you'd be capable of conversations always — you know, as we went through time to-gether. Two, the bedroom was nice, got nicer in Islay, according to my lights, at least, so I imagined that into the future, too. Three, your understanding of how deep love could go, when you responded to that waitress on Islay. That was after our marriage, of course. But most important, I felt like myself. Comfortable with myself with you. None of this completed the whole picture, naturally, but that was my list, which I tossed out after writing it. Things like that are memorized in your heart anyway — you don't need a piece of paper. Possibly we got married before we really knew each other well enough. But I never honestly felt that, and I still don't. I certainly felt we knew each other very well on Islay on our honey-moon. Very well indeed. And I think now we have to begin a sec-ond marriage within the first one, which ended pretty fast thanks to you — but also, I admit, thanks to me not considering forgive-ness. But I've been fuming. I simply refuse to hold my ignorance about you to blame. I read a Jewish proverb a few months ago, in Stefania and Izzy's library, in a book of proverbs from all over the world. It said, "I'll forgive and forget, but I'll remember." Maybe it originally pertained to some family grudge from biblical times, but I immediately applied it to us. Me toward you, I mean. Much just doesn't matter anymore. Who what where when and why doesn't matter so much anymore. I refer to the hotel room in Lon-don. What does matter is two decisions I've made. The first is, I'm naming the baby Stefania Field, and I am not soliciting your opin-ion. The name is not meant to slight my mother, and I've told my

decision to my father already and he approved. Secondly, if we de-
cide to stay married, if that's in the cards, we have to live sepa-
rately. To put it bluntly, I'd like you nearby but not in the same
house as Stefania Field and me for the three months I get off with
pay from the Dalhousie Ensemble. And I might ask for longer,
though that'd be without pay. Plus, I'm not sure the DE could get
along much longer than that without me. By the by, I asked Na-
omi Bloor in person if she ever slept with you. She's an honest per-
son. My father has invited me to stay in the main house. Stefania
Field can have the same room I had as a child. You may stay in the
guesthouse. I always find it peaceful at the estate. My mother, as
you know, is buried by the stone wall. And naturally you should
spend as much time with Stefania as possible, for her sake. It
would be an accurate understanding of the situation to consider
yourself a guest. My husband, a guest living in the guesthouse.
Oddly enough, these last months I've had more or less a fairly nor-
mal time of it, nights crying myself to sleep included, I'm not
ashamed to say. I've been to European capitals. You've been to
Parrsboro and back umpteen times, I understand. What you did
was so disappointing, there's times it unnerves me. But I'm disap-
pointing in all this too. But do you know what? We're no more dis-
appointing, I suppose, than life itself is sometimes. I realize just
now that's a sentiment I heard Stefania Tecosky express a long
time ago. But no matter, I also believe it. When thinking of you
causes me pain, I just think of Stefania Field about to be born. Just
yesterday I wrote to Stefania and Izzy overseas and told them

our daughter's name. I'm going to the doctor today. Just a regular checkup. On my own, except not really, because no pregnant woman is really on her own, is she, if you take my meaning. Anyway, David, give a second marriage some thought. As will I.

There was about a thirty-second pause, during which David stared at the tape, still turning on its spool. Then Maggie continued:

One more thing for now. Remember the strange woman on Islay, driving by with the swan in her back seat? She's settled in my mind a certain way. I know full well that on Islay she might be considered some old crazy. What did our waitress say? "She thinks that swan's her dear departed husband" — wasn't that it? But my own personal conclusion is that I envy that old woman. To love someone so deeply and with such devotion you obviously have no choice in the matter but to keep seeing him in one form or another. I would like that for myself. To be married to a man I'd eventually feel that way about.

A Phrase Favored by
Her Mother

I T WAS 6 A.M. and David lay in bed listening to the radio: ". . . the possibility of showers late in the day, especially in Cape Breton and . . ."

He dozed off, woke again around 8:15, to *Around the Province*, a show out of Truro whose host, Jeffrey Paine, took calls from listeners on this or that topic. "The words 'November' and 'heat wave' make for strange bedfellows here in Atlantic Canada," Paine said. "Yes, sir, we have children still in short sleeves lined up for the school bus. My air conditioner's acting so cool toward me, I don't even know what I did to hurt its feelings! This heat's affecting everybody. So let's hear from you. Whether your garden's still producing summer squash, or you fear it's due to a hole in the ozone layer, or whatnot, ad infinitum. The lines are open. I'm Jeffrey Paine and this is *Around the Province* for November 6, 1986, from the very center — the epicenter — the center of the center of the province, *Truh-oh!*" Paine's agenda was fairly staid, but he used to have a rock 'n' roll show and on occasion still lapsed into deejay chatter, referred to himself as "Jeffrey P," offered the odd pop-culture reference ("Well, allow me to quote one of the Canadian gods, Mr. Leonard Cohen") and so on.

Maggie had been living in the main house for nearly a week. David knew that all considerations were focused on Stefania Field, officially due in three days. William had left a letter from Stefania Tecosky on his kitchen table, which in part read, *We will arrive on November 6, hoping to be on time for the birth of Margaret and David's daughter."*

William picked up Stefania and Isador at Halifax Airport at 7 A.M. David knew they'd be at the estate any moment now. He should rouse himself, get his camera ready on the porch to chronicle their arrival, and he did sit at the edge of the bed, rubbing his face, thinking of coffee so intensely he could almost smell it brewing, though he hadn't even ground his usual morning's three cups yet. But then a call came in to *Around the Province* that caught his attention, and he sat there listening to it.

"Jeffrey," the caller said, "this is Carter Dorson in Truro."

"What's on your mind today, Carter?" Paine said.

"Well, if you read your Scripture, you might interpret a drought like we're having as a warning. We've got to change our ways. Course, no original Bible story took place in Atlantic Canada, you don't have to tell me that, but if you simply replace the names Sodom and Gomorrah with the name Halifax — what I'm saying is, *something's* put the temperature way out of whack, and how people live down there might be why we're all being punished —"

"Slow down, there, Carter," Paine said. "The fair city of Halifax?"

Then David heard William's truck. He switched off the radio, threw on his trousers, grabbed his camera, stepped onto the porch, quickly adjusted the lens and started to take photographs. William got out of the truck, reached in back and took down two suitcases, which he carried toward the house. Maggie came out smiling and embraced Stefania, then Isador, then stepped back and let them look at her recent shapeliness. Stefania kissed Maggie again. To David, Stefania and Isador looked a bit the worse for wear: it was a long journey for people their age, and according to what he'd observed on his honeymoon, the Tecoskys were already in declining health. Isador especially moved slowly. Yet they both looked tremendously pleased to be at the estate.

Through the telephoto from his porch, David photographed Isador as he kissed his own fingers, reached up and touched the mezuzah, the ancient talisman nailed to the doorframe. Then Stefania touched it, and everyone went into the house.

David sat on a porch swing for an hour or so, facing the main house, hoping for a glimpse of someone or something going on, an observer. *Now I understand John Pallismore*, he thought. But this was more: how would he get back into a life he never learned to fully occupy to begin with?

Inside the main house, Maggie prepared a lunch of roasted chicken and garlic green beans, light on the garlic. When Maggie complained that the kitchen was too stuffy, William brought in a fan. "If I feel faint," she said, "I'll drink some water and lie down. But just now I'm fine, Dad. And I'm so happy. I can hardly believe Stefania and Izzy are here!"

"Want to ask David over yet?"

"No, I do not, thank you."

This was said while Stefania and Isador were freshening up in the downstairs guest bathroom. William had brought both of their suitcases to the master bedroom upstairs.

"I never thought I'd be saying this in November," William said at lunch, "but it's warm enough to take a swim before dinner."

"That would be nice," Maggie said. "The baby's kicking up a storm. When I'm in the water, I can almost feel her relax."

Maggie on the living room sofa, Stefania and Isador upstairs, William in the guest room, each took a nap after lunch. David slept on the porch swing. At 5:30 William put on swim trunks and stepped out onto the lawn, where he found Stefania and Isador waiting, wearing their own swim outfits retrieved from a bureau drawer. Stefania's was dark blue with a frilly skirt, which William recognized as prewar vintage. Her wrinkled, small body, white hair bobby-pinned without design. Isador had on a black suit that looked at least two sizes too big. The shoulder straps loose on his bony shoulders. Maggie then appeared, stepping down from the porch in her one-piece. "A fine afternoon for a swim," she said, and the four of them set out for the pond.

"Where's David?" Isador said.

"He'll be back soon," Maggie said.

David heard voices, woke with a start, went inside and photographed Isador, Stefania, Maggie and William through the kitchen window as they passed by. Mist had begun rising in wispy, wavering columns from the water. "The bank is slippery, so be careful now," Maggie said.

"Margaret says the bank is slippery," Isador said into Stefania's better ear. Then, speechlessly, they all held hands in a daisy chain and slowly entered the water, keeping each other in balance. Observing all of this, David thought, *I'll have to invite myself.* He went into his bedroom, put on his Dalhousie University gym shorts. Everyone of importance to him was already in the pond.

Yet invited or not, David hesitated at the screen door. He listened to their drifting voices. On no evening did the entire pond mist over evenly, and now he saw the cattails at the north end had almost completely disappeared. He waited another fifteen minutes or so, then walked down. He couldn't see anyone. "Fog registered its ghostly imprimatur over the mortal life." That, a sentence from Anatole France — he knew that much, yet couldn't recall from which novel. The swans were silent, wherever they were.

David made his way into the water. Through thickening mist he heard William's voice: ". . . Naomi Bloor telephoned. Someone's brought in a gun-shot swan. She's got it eating, but one wing is useless. Naturally she wanted to know if we'd take it in."

"How can we not?" Isador said. "Of course. Yes."

"I'll let her know, then," William said.

Silence, light splashing, then Isador said, "Stefania, I confess, on the hottest days, when you were off in Parrsboro, I'd swim in this pond without you. I hope you can forgive me."

"But Isador, certainly you kept your suit on," Stefania said. "You've always been too modest that way."

"And when I went into Parrsboro?" Isador said. "On the hottest days?"

"Oh, certainly, Izzy. Of course I swam without you. But I was less modest."

Laughter; silence; and then Maggie said in a tone of excited alarm, "I have to go to the hospital now."

David said from his invisible place, "I'm here too!" But he was not heard; he might better have shouted. William helped Maggie gain dry ground, followed by Isador and Stefania. David clambered out last, but he'd been farthest out in the pond. Maggie saw him and said, "She's arriving three days early, David. That's probably my mother's impatience with things" — thinking in terms of inheritances. Maggie, William, Stefania and Isador walked to the main house. David ran to the guesthouse, put on trousers and a long-sleeve white shirt and loafers, ran out and stood by Maggie's car, which was parked next to the truck.

In a short while William emerged from the house carrying Maggie's overnight case. Maggie came out next, followed by Stefania and Isador, who shut the door behind him. Wet hair; dry, clean clothes; Maggie and her beloved entourage, not a thought in their heads except for her and Stefania Field's well-being. As things should have been. In Maggie's room, the baby quilt, in the crib made by Ezra Murry, was turned down. Maggie then crouched with a moan and slightly pained laughter into the back seat of her car. Stefania got in next to Maggie, and Isador sat in the front seat, passenger side. William looked across the hood at David, who took a step forward, then stopped. "All of us will go on ahead," William said. "You take the truck. Maybe get your camera, David. Why not take some pictures? For the album, remember?"

Maggie heard this through the open window; she approved, then felt a contraction. "We really need to go now, Dad," she said. "I mean *right* now."

"Right," William said, getting in behind the wheel and starting up the car. They drove off. David lit out for the guesthouse, got his camera, and by the time he looked again, Maggie's car was out of sight. David knew William would drive forthrightly.

David set the camera on the front seat of the truck, turned the ignition, drove to Route 2, where William stood next to Maggie's car near the mailbox. He held his right hand outstretched and began to push downward in rapid motions, gesturing David to stop the truck. David parked where the drive met Route 2, switched off the ignition, grabbed his camera and got out. He stood next to the truck. "There's room in the back seat," Maggie said through the open window.

David did not know who convinced whom and didn't care. He slid in beside Maggie. She held her right hand palm-up on her knee, and David pressed his left hand over it. They hesitated, then plaited their fingers together tightly. "Off to the next adventure," she said, a phrase favored by her mother. She closed her eyes.

The Swankeeper

November 24, 1986

Dear Margaret,

On the airplane I looked back out the window at Nova Scotia and thought about that hymn your mother liked so much, cannot for the life of me recall the title, but it included "the entire Kingdom we can see."

I want you to know that your old pop is completely devoted to Stefania Field. But here's something else came to mind on the flight. Over the past ten years there's been one in particular of the Tecoskys' swans who I've noticed is, almost without fail, either first or last onto the pond. Brave and impetuous one day, hesitant and fallen back the next. I find some familiar human tendency in this. You either can't wait or you don't want to jump in. Maybe what I'm trying to get at is, you and David couldn't wait. To get married, I mean. Then you didn't want to be. Now you've got a daughter — and there's lots of room in between those two fixed points to exist in. Sorry, Margaret, for the clumsy language, but your dad never took a poetry class in school, as you know. Enough, anyway. Maybe I'm just tired.

I'm set up in this bed & breakfast for another week and generally engaged like last time as a tourist. I had my visit with Mr. Reginald Aston, but won't see him again. A very busy man, and I doubt I've ever seen someone more dedicated to his profession. His assistant drove us down to the Thames and we toured eight different swan haunts elsewhere as well, and that was an education. Back in his office, nicely appointed, we had tea and Mr. Aston reviewed for me an average day's work. I asked him some of my questions, which he took seriously. He said he's entirely self-taught, from being given the opportunity, from observation, of course, and from books on avian medicine. He said over the years he's made mistakes, none of which directly caused a swan to lose its life, except once. Then he told me he'd taken Winston Churchill to see black swans thirty miles out of London — during the Blitz. It's a moment unknown to history, as he put it. "Just the two of us in a car like anyone's. Two soldiers along as well. Mr. Churchill gazed at the swans for some time. Their composure seemed to give him heart." To Mr. Aston's surprise, swans had long been admired by Winston Churchill, who gave Mr. Aston a pencil sketch he'd done of one. Near the end of my visit Mr. Aston took that very sketch from the wall and pointed out Churchill's personal best regards.

Kindly meet me at the airport at 10:10 on December 1.

Lord's sake, I take it the swans will be at the children's zoo by then. I look forward to home. I must see Stefania Field right away — and you, dear Margaret. And David when convenient.

Love,
Dad